A SCANDAL AT CRYSTALLINE

ROSLYN REID

Foster Embry Publishing, LLC
244 Fifth Avenue, Suite E148
New York, New York 10001
www.fosterembry.com

Printed in the United States of America

This book is dedicated to "The Most Unforgettable Character I Ever Met,"
my high school English teacher Kenny Villani,
whose influence on his students has lasted through their many lifetimes.

IN WHICH EARLY DETECTION WAS RECOMMENDED

In the charming Maine town of Finderne, on the site of an old mansion that had seen a millionaire's gruesome and unsolved murder in the 1930s, sat a sunny little café called Throw the Book. Named for its proximity to the courthouse and police station, the café was a favorite place for private detective James Early to meet up with his best friend, Police Chief Hal White. But before he could spring his usual joke on the hostess—"Is there a black guy named White here?"—he heard a loud and familiar voice cut through the hushed conversations and clinking dishes.

"Early, get your black ass over here."

From his seat beside a floor-to-ceiling window, the Chief waved his fork at Early before plunging it into a small mountain of pasta. Early's long legs sauntered over the creaking floorboards as he basked in the intoxicating smells of freshly baked bread and frying bacon. "Taking a break, Hal?"

Hal fist bumped him. "Gotta. This business is murder."

"Are you ever gonna stop telling the same jokes you did

when we were twerps in New Jersey? That stale crap will ruin my lunch."

"You want ruined? I can do ruined."

Oh shit, Early thought, *now I got him started. After all these years I should know better.*

Hal seized the metal cheese grater from the tabletop. "I worked this murder as a detective in Philly—"

"Ah, Chief, could I please order something before you begin?"

"Of course. Jerry!" The Chief signaled the waiter, who hustled over with a menu.

Early waved the menu away. When Hal started one of his cop-shop yarns—and there was no stopping him—the smart money was on not eating. "Just a cuppa, please, Jerry. The usual—black, no sugar."

"I'll have another bottle of Riverdriver Beer," said Hal.

"Comin' right up." Jerry rushed off.

"Didn't you hear about that new study linking coffee to heart attacks?" the Chief asked before emptying his beer.

Early rolled his eyes. "Thanks. Until now I didn't think ruining a cup of coffee was possible."

"Well, you did say I should ruin your lunch. So, about that murder . . ."

Early braced for the worst, but he was too optimistic.

"This perp lived with her boyfriend, see, and one day she decided to try some younger meat of the female variety. So, she picked up a fifteen year old girl at the local crack-head park, dumb enough to believe this woman would be her meal ticket. But her 'meal ticket' had no job, no income, and no money—she and her boyfriend were living off his welfare check." Hal stopped chewing and leaned forward. "Know what the perp did then?"

"I have to admit I'm a detective without a clue."

"She moved her little hoochie right into their house. Now there were *three* of them living off the boyfriend's welfare check."

"The boyfriend was okay with this? He sounds like a real loser."

"He wasn't getting anything from the kid, either," the Chief went on. "One night they all got drunk or stoned or whatever, and the two ladies come to the conclusion that the boyfriend has become somewhat inconvenient. They decide to kill him; but girls just wanna have fun, right? Their idea of fun is to torture him." The Chief picked up the cheese grater again. "And how do you think they did it?"

"Did what? The torture? The murder? I give up."

Hal leaned forward and held the grater close to his ample cheek. "They held him down," he hissed, "and the perp took a cheese grater just like this one, and—"

"Stop!" Early threw both hands out in front of him.

The Chief put down the grater, sat back, and flashed an evil grin. "Squeamish?"

"No," Early lied, "my heart attack is here."

Jerry returned with Early's coffee and the Chief's beer, and then scurried off. He wanted no more of Hal's perp stories, either.

Early reminisced as he rubbed the scar a childhood sledding accident had left on his chin. "I think I know just how the guy felt."

The Chief dug into his pasta with renewed gusto. "That's just a small sample of what we folks in the trenches see. The general populace has no idea—"

"Even though you keep telling them about it?" Early watched Hal shovel in the pasta. Gruesome cop tales seemed to enhance the Chief's appetite and he wanted to get to the point of this meeting before Hal started another one. "What do you have on Chandler Hammond's disappearance last month?"

"He's a rich guy who skipped town with his girlfriend. What else is there to know?"

"Not everybody believes that."

Hal grated more cheese onto his pasta. "You mean his sister, Honoria? She's been a real pest down at the station."

"Always do what you're best at."

"She's convinced her brother met up with some kinda sinister fate. Probably because their father was kidnapped, but that was a long time ago."

"She told me she had this feeling—"

Hal astonished Early by putting down his fork. "So, you weren't kidding this morning when you said she called you yesterday?"

"I was as serious as a car crash."

Hal cleared his throat and wiped his mouth on a napkin. "Great Hitchens' ghost! Are you taking her case? You really want to work this dog?"

Early did a face plant into his hands on the table. "You told her to call me, and now you say her case is a dog."

Hal leaned over the table and rapped Early with his knuckles. "Hey," Early yelled. "Don't ruin my 'do—I spent all morning getting the frizz out of my 'fro."

"I never have that problem." The Chief snickered as he ran his hand over his bald head. "But wake up and smell the beer. The guy left on his own. Guys as rich as Hammond do whatever they want. Honoria's idea is plain crazy."

Early looked up. "We've been friends since high school. Have I ever been suckered into anything crazy?"

Hal raised his eyebrows, pursed his lips, folded his hands over his ample belly, and rocked back in his chair. Finally, he said, "Maybe you have crazier drugs now?"

"You know I never did drugs."

"Oh yeah? So, what we smoked behind the vo-tech school's dynamo after the prom was just regular cigarettes?"

"Well, no . . ."

"Good, otherwise, I'd feel cheated."

"But why do you think her case is a dog? Is there any good reason why I shouldn't take it?"

"You'd be wasting your time." Hal pointed his fork at Early. "First, Honoria can be hell to deal with. Second, Hammond's probably busy doing the nasty with his girlfriend and does *not* want his nosy sister tracking him down. And last, you must agree that one less financier in our town is not a bad thing."

Early had already considered the same reasons and found them unpersuasive. "Try swallowing your food before you rant or it might kill you. Then I would have a funny cop story for the guys at the station."

"I realize this is my fault," Hal said after swallowing a bite of bread, "but I didn't think she'd actually call you."

"You didn't? Are you sure you were talking to Honoria?"

"Who else could be such an accomplished pain in the ass?"

Early figured he'd spare Hal his answer for now.

"I call her Lady Massa," Hal said with a wink. "Do you know Honoria has a street named after her? It's called 'One Way'."

Early held his nose to keep coffee from bursting out. Regaining his composure, he said, "I agree that fewer financiers are better. But she wants me to look into his disappearance and that's how I pay the bills. Besides, I need the work—I have this teenager who eats video games for breakfast, along with all the food in the house."

"At least you have only one," Hal sympathized. "I've got

two, and the other two are approaching teenage at warp speed." He sopped up more tomato sauce. "You're right, Honoria can afford to piss away her money. Why shouldn't you take advantage of that?"

"I'm trying. What can you tell me about Hammond?"

The Chief sat back in thought. "I never saw him much except at official functions, like Eggs and Issues."

"The Chamber of Commerce breakfasts? You go to those?"

"Don't have to, but I like to get my face in the place. Someday I might want to run for something." Hal smiled like a Cheshire cat, flashing a gold tooth.

"Why would you wanna do lots more work for lots less money?"

Hal's smile faded. "You're the only Mainer I know who has just one job."

"Besides yourself."

Hal sighed. "Let's get back to Hammond. I'd see him at some event, say hello, chat a bit. He's a hustler, always looking for investors. And his pitch is not at all subtle."

"Did he ever hit you up to invest in the Crystalline Art Distributorship?"

"His company? Of course. He tried to impress me by telling me it's a ten-million-dollar company. He didn't seem to get that anybody on a policeman's salary isn't gonna pop him a bundle." Hal sneered. "But he and I are only passing acquaintances. We did do a brief investigation just to shut Honoria up, but my men found that no one seems to know much about Hammond other than his sales pitch for Crystalline."

"Crystalline was his only source of income?"

"We found no record of a relationship with any other company, either by employment or ownership. I had never considered looking into his revenue sources since I wasn't interested in investing. I think he and Honoria inherited their money, and our usual informants haven't linked him to any illicit activities. If his income is legit, it doesn't concern me. He says Crystalline handles high-end art and antiquities. Seems to be a lot of money in that."

"You knew about his Iraqi girlfriend?"

Hal chuckled. "Who doesn't? Even his wife knows. His girlfriend's family was tight with Saddam, and Hammond procured antiquities through them. When our boys blew up Iraq, the family figured getting the hell out was prudent. Have you talked to his wife yet?"

"No. Have you?"

"Yeah, but it was more of a conversation than an interrogation. Regardless of what Honoria thinks, this isn't a missing person case. The guy's of legal age, he's financially independent, and it's a free country. We didn't uncover anything suspicious; therefore, our position is that he can come and go as he pleases. Apparently, his sister involved the police because she doesn't believe he would just leave."

"Because that's his wife's story," said Early, "and it was obvious from her phone call that she hates his wife. You uncovered no signs of foul play?"

"We tried, but records show his cell phone was still active after his disappearance."

"Somebody could have stolen his phone."

"True, except the calls were all to his wife. Why would somebody steal Hammond's phone just to call his wife?"

"Maybe she hired a hit man and he was reporting in?"

"Great Hitchens' ghost, Early, you come up with the damnedest ideas."

"I like to consider all possibilities."

"And impossibilities too?"

"Impossibilities merely take a little longer to prove. Do you know what tower the phone was pinging off?"

"No."

"Did you ask his wife about the calls?"

"We didn't receive the records until after we interviewed her. By then we figured the phone calls, along with his Bentley being found in the airport parking lot, were enough proof that he's alive. We considered running his credit cards, but his wife said hers is the only one they have."

"No company card?"

"Nada."

"What about credit bureau reports?"

"No credit cards or loans, either in his name or the company's. The information the bureaus had on him was several years old and they had none on Crystalline."

"That sounds more suspicious than his disappearance. How does anybody conduct business without credit?"

"Beats me." Hal took another swig of beer. "We even did an informal sweep of his mansion but found no bloodstains or anything else out of the ordinary. His personal stuff is gone—laptop, cell phone, car keys. His wife said he cleaned out the safe too." The Chief wiped his mouth and belched happily.

"He could have flown somewhere if his car was in the airport parking lot."

"Maybe. We did check for plane tickets, but I'm sure his Iraqi girlfriend knows where to obtain phony IDs."

"Did you process his car?"

"It was gone. His wife sold it after she had it towed home."

"Towed? There was no spare key?"

"They're gone too. His wife said he keeps the car keys

with him because he doesn't want anybody else driving his precious Bentley. Such a jerk."

"Hell, I'd feel the same way if I paid that kind of money for a car."

"Chump change for him." The Chief scraped up the last of his pasta. "Besides, if he left his car behind, why the hell would he care who's driving it?"

"He would if he plans on coming back. His disappearance sounds more intentional."

"That's why I say this case is a dog. I'll be glad to help you out all I can, bruh, but don't expect any miracles."

"Did you question his friends and associates?"

Hal shrugged. "He hardly seems to have any. You might try interviewing the other Chamber or country club members, but I doubt they'd be helpful. Aside from whatever he's telling people to part them from their cash, he's not very forthcoming."

Usually, Mainers didn't need to be forthcoming because everybody in town knew everything anyway. If nobody knew much about Hammond, Early figured the financier liked it that way. The Hammond family played close to the vest.

"Did you talk to anybody at his company?" Early asked.

"There is nobody at his company."

"What do you mean?"

"My understanding is that Hammond ran the business on his own out of his home."

Early stared. "His company had no second in command?"

"Yeah, surprised me too," Hal said.

"Your investigation seems thorough, despite having no reason to investigate. Why is Honoria bitching?"

"She didn't like the results."

Early killed his coffee and grabbed his hat. "I'll head back to my office, set up an appointment with Hammond's wife, and see Honoria later."

Hal licked his lips and stacked his dirty dishes. "Lunch is on *your* expense account this time."

"What? All I had was a cuppa."

Hal made sad eyes in faux sympathy. "Like I said, this is no longer police business. We closed the case. Aside from a few statements and some other minuscule information, the guy's official file is full of a whole lot of nothing." He gave Early the eye. "And I do have a boss who expects me to justify my expenses."

"News to me." Early scowled. "I'll pay up this time, but thanks for your non-help, bruh. I'll go down to the station now to check out his file for myself."

"I'll call ahead to let them know you're coming." Hal flipped out his phone. "But you have to admit, I'm rarely no help to you. By the way, as long as you're paying, tell Jerry to bring me one of those delicious blueberry whoopie pies when you leave."

"Ah, the state treat. By all means." Early turned and roared as loud as he could, "Jerry, Chief Chubby here wants a blueberry whoopie pie, pronto."

2

IN WHICH EARLY HOLDS ALL THE CARDS

Early walked into the waiting room he shared with the psychic across the hall from his office. The lights were off and, in the gloom, he saw a shadowy figure lurking in the hallway. He dropped to a crouch and pulled his weapon. "Freeze! Identify yourself."

"Relax, Dickless Tracy, it's me—Amber."

He exhaled and holstered his gun. "Sorry, neighbor. What happened to the lights?"

"Another power failure. Guess that's the penalty for having an office on the cheap side of town. I was just starting with a client, but it scared her into leaving."

"A power failure is scarier than the future?"

"She said she thought it was a sign of the apocalypse and she didn't want to be left behind." Amber snapped her gum. "Hey, I have some time on my hands now. How about a tarot reading?"

"In the dark?"

"That just adds ambiance."

They walked down the hall to Amber's windowless office, as dark inside as a catacomb. Early handed her his flashlight so she could fetch a pair of candles in ornate silver holders from a corner cabinet. After lighting them and placing them on her reading table, she pulled a tarot deck from a squeaky drawer. Early sat down as candlelight flickered across the swirling designs of the metaphysical posters on the walls.

"What's your question, Early?"

"I'm looking for Chandler Hammond. Can you tell me where he is?"

"The rich guy who ran off with his girlfriend?"

"Yeah, him. Got any insight?"

"We'll see. You know, some readers tell a client what they want to hear." She shook the deck at Early. "I try to tell them the truth."

"Of course. Will it be the usual procedure, even when the reading is on someone else?"

"As long as you don't ask questions like 'What is he thinking?' I consider mind-reading an invasion of privacy, and I very firmly inform a client that the best way to find out what somebody is thinking is to ask them. If they don't like it and they try to press me—end of reading." She handed him the deck.

"It's been a while. Refresh my memory."

"Hold your question as clearly as possible in your mind."

Find Chandler Hammond. Where is Chandler Hammond? "Now shuffle?"

"Give them a good one. Concentrate on your question."

He shuffled like a card shark in Vegas, startling Amber with his rough treatment of her deck, but he'd show those cards who's boss. "Now what?"

She took the deck and placed it face down on the table,

fanning it out with her long red fingernails. "Keep thinking about your question."

"You're not doing the usual spread?"

"This is my fast and dirty method. Three cards only."

Early closed his eyes and focused on Chandler Hammond. *Tell me where he is, tell me where he is.* When he felt ready, he said, "Go ahead."

"Open your eyes, pull out three cards, and turn them face up."

He opened his eyes. His hand hovered over the cards, and then quickly picked out three cards to flip over.

Amber stared at the cards for such a long time that Early finally asked, "Well? What do they say?"

She placed her ring-encrusted fingers atop the first card. "The three of swords. Some readers say this card means a broken heart due to a third party. I typically read it as treachery, being stabbed in the heart—or the back—but right now I'm getting that broken-heart vibe too. Three swords can also indicate that two people, not just one, caused the broken heart."

"There do seem to be three principals in this case: Hammond, his wife, and his girlfriend," Early said. "His sister Honoria could be broken-hearted but that would make four. Maybe the card refers to Hammond's wife? I haven't found out yet how broken-hearted she is."

"Interpretation is always fluid, affected by the influence of the surrounding cards."

Early grinned. "Just like people."

"Too true. Honoria was here to consult me, you know."

"She asked you to find her brother?"

"Yes. This card came up in her reading too; along with one indicating a dark-haired woman who was hiding something. I told her the dark-haired woman might be causing the broken heart or Chandler Hammond might have broken *her* heart. Meanings vary with clients."

"Sounds confusing."

"In confusion there is profit." Amber snickered.

"What else did you tell her?"

"Nothing. She didn't like her reading, so she got up and left—without paying me."

"Now we know how she got all that money. What else do you see here?"

Amber licked her shiny red lips as she ran her finger along the white border of the second card. "The seven of swords, sometimes called the 'Sneak Thief.' And he's good at what he does—seven is the number of success."

"As in seven come eleven? How well I remember those nights on my Air Force base." Early chuckled. "Is gender irrelevant? Could the card mean Hammond's girlfriend successfully stole him?"

"You catch on pretty quick. Ever thought of becoming a phone psychic?"

"It helps to be somewhat psychic in my line of business. Sometimes to be a bit of a psychiatrist too." He drummed his fingers on the table. "This is fascinating, Amber, but you haven't told me anything I don't know."

"Do you *know* Hammond and his girlfriend ran off together?"

"No. But a card reading's not gonna prove they did."

"It can provide corroboration."

"True, but . . . there's something I don't get." He pursed his lips. "If the first card, the broken heart due to a third party, means his girlfriend stole him, why would the Sneak Thief show up and tell you the same thing?"

"Perhaps for emphasis. Or maybe he wasn't what was stolen. Maybe his wife is *glad* he left." Amber winked and looked at the card again. "But the Sneak Thief refers to property, not matters of the heart. Maybe Hammond and the dark-haired woman were in on something shady together." She paused to pull on her tattooed ear. "And sometimes the real meaning isn't apparent until long after the reading is over."

"What the hell kind of fortune-telling is that? By then it's too late."

Amber laughed. "I reveal hidden influences rather than telling fortunes. And hidden influences usually stay hidden if somebody wants it that way."

"Don't I know it. What hidden influences do you see in that last card?"

"The six of pentacles? Somebody who's careless with money. They flash the cash to give the impression they have more than they do. But six is the number of rewards, which means someday the party will be over and they'll get what's coming to them."

Early pondered this. "From what I've heard, Hammond does like to emphasize his revenue flow. But is running off with his girlfriend what's coming to him? I could live with that kind of karma."

Amber waved her hand, rings and bracelets flashing in the candlelight. "To us, he seems to be sitting pretty, but we don't know where he is or what he's doing. Most of the cards in this reading are swords, which indicate mental turmoil. His girlfriend might have stolen his money and dumped him. Or worse."

Early thought this was a creepy thing to say—but saying creepy things might be part of Amber's business. He tilted his chair back, pulled out a pack of nicotine gum, unwrapped a stick, and popped it into his mouth. "What's the bottom line? The cards didn't really give us an answer."

"Everything seems up in the air. Shall we try a full reading tomorrow?"

He chuckled. "Do you suggest that to all your clients?"

"Only when readings are this vague. I'm curious about this situation too."

"Can't we clarify things right now?"

"Better to let the cards cool off a bit."

Early picked up the three cards, stared at them, and tossed them back down. "You expect me to believe this stuff? What kind of bullshit is this?"

Amber smiled sweetly. "What kind of bullshit would you like it to be?"

"I would like to find Chandler Hammond."

She bowed her head. "I know you're sincere, but there's the danger of reading too much into the cards. For instance"—she sifted through the deck, pulled out a card, and placed it on the table—"here's the Queen of Wands. My job is to help you discover what the card's symbolism means to you. This picture includes several solar references: sunflowers, obviously; and lions have been a sun symbol since the ancient Sumerians. Wands indicate heat or fire, even passion. But look at what's in front of the Queen's throne."

"That little black cat?"

"I've seen readers bend over backward to attribute major symbolism to that cat. Some say since it's black, it represents bad luck—"

"Hey," Early growled.

Amber laughed. "Sorry, but that superstition way predates the Civil Rights Act. Other readers suggest the cat symbolizes the Queen's animal nature. I remember one who stretched the sun link to the max by calling it a baby lion. You see how easily one can misread symbolism?"

"Seems so."

"The truth is"—she lowered her voice—"the cat belonged to the model who posed for the painting this card is based on. The cat sat quite placidly—and you might say, regally—impressing the artist, Pamela Smith, enough to include her in the portrait."

Early loved such debunking stories. "There goes the *DaVinci Code*. Sounds like you need to be more careful about doing readings than I thought."

"I have enough experience presenting bad news to clients without freaking them out that I could be a diplomat. A good reader should always offer a positive approach to a difficult situation."

"Or else you don't get paid." He chuckled. "I know from my divorce cases. Did I ever mention the client who called me a liar, kicked me, walked out of my office, and never paid me? All because I took photos of her husband going to a motel with another woman—which is what she hired me to find out."

Amber giggled. "Even if the news isn't bad, you might be telling the client something they don't want to hear or not telling them what they do want to hear. Either way, they don't want to pay for something they don't like."

"The perils of the modern-day fortune-teller."

"Beats being an ancient fortune-teller. Back then, if the king didn't like his reading, off with your head."

"Good approach for modern-day weather forecasters."

Amber gasped. "They would all be extinct."

He smiled and leaned over the table. "As much as I'm enjoying this conversation, I'd still like some insight on Hammond's whereabouts."

"Let me try a different technique." Amber closed her eyes and meditated, and then frowned. "This is very odd."

"What is?"

"I asked the universe to show me where he is, but I get no indication of a place. All I see is the color red. A bright, vibrant, beautiful red."

"Like a red flag?" He laughed. "Maybe Honoria's spirit is hanging around here waving one in your face."

Amber paused, and then began bouncing up and down. "Wait, something else is coming through. It looks like . . . a cabin in the woods."

Early was glad her eyes were closed and she couldn't see him cover up a smirk. The exotic sights and smells of Amber's world were beginning to make him giddy. "A red cabin in the woods?"

Amber opened her big blue eyes and frowned. "Don't be a wise ass. That red color burst over me like a water balloon." Her eyes shone as she held up her hands to the sky. "A luscious, glorious, intoxicating red."

"I'd love to know the meaning of that."

"Me too. My clients don't allow me to say 'I don't know.' And I hate dead ends."

"You're not alone. That's the whole problem—this case might be a dead end."

Amber replaced the deck in the table drawer. "Sorry I couldn't be more help. You might need it; Honoria can be very difficult. She doesn't necessarily believe the facts."

"And she might not pay me, either." They both laughed, even though Early didn't think spending lots of time on a case for no money was funny. Reminded about time, he held his watch up to a candle. "My son should be home from school by now. Thanks for the reading, and please let me know if you think of anything else concerning Hammond."

"I will. And tell your sweet son I said hello."

"Sure thing." He winked and closed the door behind him.

As he walked down the hall, he contemplated Amber's vision of a cabin in the woods. The Chief had mentioned that Amber always saw a cabin in the woods when she worked on a case for them. Didn't she realize that almost every Mainer with some discretionary income or talent at swinging a hammer owned a cabin in the woods? Duh.

3

IN WHICH EARLY GETS A LITTLE CHRISTMAS

Early perused the slender Hammond file at a table in the cop shop. The file made him think of the old Peggy Lee song, "Is That All There Is?" The police had done a respectable investigation, but there wasn't much to find. The situation still smelled like Hammond had left voluntarily.

Then his eye fell upon a curious statement in the police report: "Miss Hammond states she is concerned because of the incident involving her father when the family lived in Massachusetts."

Early pulled out his phone and punched in Hal's number. "Do you have any information on this 'incident' involving Honoria's father in Massachusetts? That was his kidnapping, right?" he asked the Chief.

"We've got a copy of everything the police down there have. I thought maybe both situations were similar enough to lend her concerns some credibility, but I concluded that the only relevance her father's case had was to traumatize Honoria. Although I can't say her fears are totally unfounded—the Hammonds are still filthy rich, so the problem could recur."

"This is intriguing. Where's the file?"

"In the basement in dead storage."

"Great. I just love spiders." Early hung up, headed for the basement door, clattered down the rickety stairs, and walked over to one of the huge old file cabinets. After checking the labels on the drawers and wrestling one open, he riffled through folders and pulled out a very thick one marked "Hammond." He sat down at a table, swept off the dust, and opened the file.

The contents were a conglomeration of police reports, hand-written notes, and newspaper articles. He decided to start with the police reports.

I, Officer McDonald Torrey, was notified via radio by central dispatch of an emergency call at Thirteen Elm Street. Mrs. Celeste Hammond had called in at 7:30 a.m. to report her husband McKinley Hammond's car idling at the end of their driveway without seeing him anywhere in the vicinity. I responded to the scene and found the car had stopped idling due to running out of gas.

Wow. They must have had quite a long driveway if the car ran that long without anybody noticing.

I secured the bottom of the driveway with crime scene tape and drove up to the house to interview Mrs. Hammond,

who was very distraught. No other occupants were in the
house. Two minor children were in school at the time. I
called in to dispatch to request a cruiser for their transport
from the school back to Thirteen Elm Street.

Early perused the diagram Officer Torrey had drawn. The
car was angled in the driveway and a folded newspaper in a
bag was on the ground next to it. Clearly, McKinley
Hammond had been snatched when he got out of his car to
fetch the newspaper. Early went back to the narrative.

Mrs. Hammond stated that she is a homemaker and was at
home all morning but saw or heard no disturbances
outside. I canvassed the other three houses on the street
and found no one home. At 9:05 a.m., I conducted a field
interview with Mr. Kendall Joseph, who was walking his
dog. He stated that around 7:00 a.m. he had passed a white
van parked on the street, which he took for a lawn service
vehicle. I returned to my cruiser and requested a detective
to be dispatched to the scene.

Early flipped through the rest of the report, and then examined some of the other documents in the file. He was
impressed by the thoroughness of the local police on the
case—there was a thick stack of every kind of documentation imaginable.

He pulled out one of the newspaper articles. The headline kicked off in the usual fashion: "Horrifying Incident on Elm Street."

Corporate executive McKinley Hammond was abducted from his driveway early yesterday morning. Police have his family under twenty-four-hour guard and the children are not allowed to return to school. At this point, there are no ransom demands and no suspects.

No ransom demands? Early wondered what the kidnappers had been waiting for. Demands for ransom were usually issued within hours of the crime. He flipped to the next article, dated several days later.

Last night McKinley Hammond's family received a ransom note from his abductors, who are calling themselves the Malamoosic Liberation Front. Police say the group is demanding one million dollars and an airplane to take them to Nicaragua before they will return Hammond. The note claims the money will be used to fund the "revolution."

Early found no further documentation of any kind for about a week's time. Then the story picked up fast and furious with a lengthy newspaper article about the kidnappers' capture and Hammond's rescue.

The note instructed the family to place the money into a
brown paper bag and leave the bag in a certain trash can
in Greenway Park. After Mrs. Hammond did so, police
kept the trash can under surveillance and arrested the
abductors when they showed up to retrieve the money.

Early rolled his eyes. No wonder their ransom demand took
such a long time; they were amateurs. Even worse than
being kidnapped is being kidnapped by dumbasses. The
Malamoosic Liberation Front sounded like the kind of clue-
less sixties radical group that went around blowing up
buildings for no reason other than to make a nuisance of
themselves. He returned to the article.

During the week, the police department stopped an
unusually large number of speeders who turned out to be
FBI agents chasing down sightings of the white van
supposedly used by the kidnappers. When the FBI
complained about the traffic stops, the local police
department said they had never been informed that
federal agents were on the case or even in the area. The
police thought they were apprehending the usual traffic
violators. No white van was ever located in connection
with the case.

Early chuckled about the infighting and the fact that the
white van had been a red herring, so to speak. That
phantom white van seemed to turn up in many cases he and

the Finderne police had handled. What is it about white vans?

He skipped to the conclusion of the case:

> After their interrogation, the abductors led detectives to where they had chained Hammond to a steam pipe in the basement of an abandoned school building. Police said he was unharmed but could have used a shower and a good meal. He was returned to his family, who presumably took care of the matter.

The article ended with the details about the charges and the trial date, and a picture of McKinley Hammond reuniting with his family. His wife was crying into his chest. Honoria was at the bottom of the picture, clinging to her father's leg, while Chandler held onto one of his arms. Apparently, the story had gone cold after that because it was the last newspaper clipping in the file.

Early wondered why the group had targeted Hammond. Victims weren't usually chosen at random. He had even heard of a case where a group had broken into the headquarters of some high-profile activists supported by the rich and famous to obtain addresses of the wealthy people who had signed their petitions. But there was no indication the Hammond family had a lot of money—back in those days, corporate executives weren't making obscene salaries.

Then Early came upon the final document in the case file, a police report submitted by the detective in charge. While interrogating a member of the Malamoosic Liberation Front, he had discovered that the "Front" was really the owners of a landscaping company who claimed Hammond had gone deadbeat on several thousand dollars he owed them, and they decided kidnapping him would be the best way to get paid. Early shook his head. Even though the Hammonds sounded like skinflints, the perps were still a bunch of dumbasses for using such an absurd approach to obtain redress.

The report said because the family felt like they had become a target for criminals, they had decided to leave Massachusetts and relocate to Maine. That explained how Chandler Hammond and his Crystalline Art Distributorship had ended up in the unlikely location of Finderne.

Reading about the case, Early felt like a character in an old movie. He closed the file, replaced it in the ancient cabinet, and went upstairs. During his stint in the police station's windowless dungeon, the rain had come down in buckets. He puddle-jumped through the parking lot to his big brown Chevy Caprice—a former cop car he had snagged for a good price at a police auction—started it up and reached into his pocket for some nicotine gum. To his horror, the pack was empty. This called for an emergency visit to the nearest quickie mart. He hit the gas.

Cruising along the gloomy and deserted country road gave him a chance to review the information he had amassed on the Hammond case. Honoria thought everyone was way too eager to believe her brother had tired of gray Maine winters—or of his wife—and followed the sun. In her mind, even the police had taken the easy way out.

Maybe they did. Maybe they have real crimes to solve and they don't think this is one of them.

Early hadn't minded the gray Maine winters until his wife left him and their son to move to Oregon last year. He missed lying beside her warm body on brisk nights and snuggling together to chase away snowy morning chills. So, yeah, he could see taking off for a tropical paradise with his hot exotic girlfriend . . . if he had one. Hell, a guy with Hammond's money could have several.

On the other hand, there was her father's kidnapping. Like father, like son? Had Chandler run afoul of another desperate contractor while carrying on the family deadbeat tradition?

The Caprice hissed along in the drizzle, passing church spires and neat little white houses, which soon gave way to rugged countryside. Tall pines swayed in the wind, sheltering the occasional deer or turkeys foraging in the tangled brush. Rain blurred the distant mountains, their snowy peaks standing out against the dark vegetation that flowed down their sides.

Early ignored the lush scenery and native wildlife to pursue his latest idea. Did Hammond have multiple girl-friends? That sounded like trouble. Was he hiding them from each other? Like some kind of . . . love quadrangle?

Hammond's ditching a supposedly multi-million-dollar art business to slip away like a thief in the night did seem suspicious. On the other hand, people don't announce their intention to disappear. But if he and his girlfriend just wanted to avoid a nasty winter, why wait until it was almost over? And most importantly, why hadn't he designated someone to run his company?

He abandoned his pride and joy, just like my wife did.

The solitude of the open road usually facilitated Early's reasoning, but trying to pin down a plausible motive for Hammond's disappearance made his brain hurt. Maybe the cops had overlooked something. After he interviewed Hammond's wife he could—

What the hell?

Early stood on the brakes and the car fishtailed to a stop. A dim creature was moving erratically in the gloom where the road met the edge of the woods. Bicycle? Moose? UFO?

He inched the Caprice along the shoulder, peering into the drizzle as the hazy form approached. Suddenly, a jogger in a bright red Santa suit burst from the chilly mist. Early exhaled. The sight wasn't unusual for Maine, although it seemed a bit bizarre for April. He cranked down his window and yelled, "Are you okay?"

Santa Jogger nodded, gave a cheery wave, and dashed down the darkening highway.

"Well . . . happy holidays, I guess." Early drove on, bemused. *Should I notify the cops? A Santa suit could be a good disguise for a heist.*

Nah. If he reported a suspicious Santa to the county mounties, they would just laugh their asses off. Sure, they might say, we know about him, he breaks into houses at Christmas every year. And you'll never believe how he gets in—right down the chimney.

Ah, the hell with it. He'd seen stranger things in Maine, and would again. Anyway, the jogging Santa didn't have a toy sack, where would he stash the take? But then there was that fat belly . . .

Early needed to get to the quickie mart before closing time. He hit the gas, dismissing the jogger as odd but harmless. *Am I too suspicious? Of the Hammond case too? Should I just relax about taking it on and see where it leads?*

The first thing he noticed when he arrived at the quickie mart was they had changed their sign to reflect the season: "Ammo, beer & prom gowns."

Sometimes Early thought Maine had grown a little too comfortable with its own weirdness.

4

IN WHICH THE GENERATIONS GAP

"Freeze, sonofabitch, or you're dead meat."

Early hit the deck. Who the hell was in his house? He peered up the front staircase but saw only darkness.

"On the ground, you bastard!"

Say what? He was already on the ground. Who could he have pissed off badly enough for them to break into his house and threaten his life?

"I said shut up, I ain't listening to no more of your shit."

Shut up? He hadn't said anything. Oh, wait . . .

He scrambled to his feet and bellowed, "Tikki, turn off that goddamn video game and get down here for supper."

His little black cat made a desperate dash under the couch. *Oops, I didn't mean to scare her.* He didn't mean to cuss in front of his son either, although the kid probably heard much worse from those damn video games.

"Aww, Daaaad . . ." Tikki's voice cascaded down the stairs like a waterfall of fine whine.

"Don't 'aw Dad' me." Early tossed his shabby Lieutenant Columbo trench coat over a chair and flopped onto the couch.

Tikki stomped down the stairs, pissing and moaning, his red high-top sneakers landing on each tread with a loud thud.

"Being thirteen's a real bitch, huh?" Early jeered, ignoring his resolve not to cuss. "You spend too much time with those damn video games."

"But, Dad, they don't do me no harm. My grades are awesome and I never get in trouble."

"Back in my day, we'd play on teams for free. Now I have to spend big money on games that teach you how to cuss, steal cars, and beat people up."

"Dad, really?" Hands on hips, Tikki glared as if he were the Dad. "I have no wish, want, or desire to beat anybody up; I have no idea how to steal a car; and I knew how to cuss long before I ever played a video game."

"*Long* before?" Early laughed. "You're just a microchip off the old block."

The boy raised his arms. "MC Tikki, that's me."

"Emcee? Of what?"

Tikki rolled his eyes. "No, no, Micro Chip Tikki. Off the old silicon block."

Early started to feel like much too old of a block to keep up with this young chip. He patted the couch and tried to divert the conversation from technology. "What did you learn in school today?"

A slow grin spread across Tikki's face, like sunrise streaming over a mountain peak. Bouncing onto the couch, he cried, "I learned the first rule of yoga class."

"You seem a little too excited," Early said warily. "But I'll bite—what is it?"

"Farts happen."

Early's face sank into his big hands.

"But wait, there's more—know what pose you'll be in when they do?" the boy cried, laughing all over.

Early looked up. "Probably lotus. Then you'd get the full effect."

Tikki frowned. "No fair, that was *my* joke."

"Life is unfair." Early leaned back.

Tikki perked up. "But I've got some good news. We got a letter from Mom today."

"From her Yurt-ness, Queen of the Sasquatch?" Early's snarky tone softened when he saw Tikki's face fall. "Now, son, you know I'm just kidding."

Tikki fidgeted with his fingers, eyes downcast. "Are you?"

Early pulled his son closer and rubbed his shoulder. "Tikki . . . I know it hurts, but we have to face facts: your mother said she needed to seek out her True Essence as an artist. I even admire her—somewhat—for having the courage to follow her dreams. But that doesn't mean I have to like it. And you don't either." He pursed his lips. "I don't know why she went off to the wilds of Oregon, though. What's wrong with Maine? She could seek her True Essence in the wilds right here."

"*Boring* wilds." Tikki moped. "I'd rather read the *Wall Street Journal*."

While he thought it commendable for teenagers to enjoy reading business news, Early didn't see how any kid could find the wilds boring. Maybe he should have enrolled Tikki in the Scouts. The ghost stories his troop told around crackling campfires in the dark woods had been anything but boring.

"There's lots to do in the Maine woods. Hiking, hunting, kayaking on the Allagash, snowshoeing, skiing the Huts and Trails, ice fishing—"

"Dad. Cool it. You don't like to do any of that stuff."

Early shut his mouth, and then tried again. "Well, summer is almost here. You always enjoyed being outdoors and planting flowers . . ."

He stopped short of blurting out "with your mother," but it was too late—his son knew what he hadn't said. They shifted on the couch in awkward silence, and then Tikki whispered, "Dad? Do you think she's going to come back?"

Early scowled and shook his head. "I dunno, son. Some things you think will never change. And then . . . they do."

Tikki's golden eyes searched his father's face. "Can we stop that?"

"No. All we can do is enjoy what we have while we have it. Nothing is permanent; mountains wear down and seas dry up." He smiled. "But you can see your mother's artwork on her website and she corresponds with us. Doesn't that help?"

"Yeah, but I send her a lot more texts and emails than she sends me."

"Hell, I don't get any." Another oops—Early saw that his remark didn't help matters.

Clients had cried on Early's broad shoulders over the years. He could handle that, but dealing with the same thing from his son was different. He tried stroking Tikki's back. "Be persistent. Persistence pays." *Hell, it probably pays better than detective work.* "We got a letter from her today, right? Or *you* got one."

Early felt ashamed of his jealous dig when he saw Tikki frown. He couldn't seem to stop putting his size thirteen foot in his mouth. "Uh, I mean, how did you feel when you read her letter?"

"There wasn't much to feel anything about."

"Well, what did she say?"

"I'll show you." Tikki cartwheeled to the dining room

table, grabbed his mother's letter, and jumped onto the couch. "She's hiking, horseback riding, writing, and painting. She went to the beach and read a mystery."

"Nothing she couldn't have done here." Early struggled to hide his bitterness, putting on a cheery face for Tikki's sake. "Nothing about coming back home?"

"No. She says she loves us, same as always."

"You believe her, don't you?"

His son stared at the letter. "Do you believe her?"

"Of course." Early wondered if he really did. Or if Tikki believed *him*.

"I guess I do, too, then." Tikki stared out the bay window. "Do you think that was the real reason why she left?"

"I don't know, son. Maybe Oregon has better beaches than we do. Maybe she overdosed on Thoreau: run off to the woods, become a hermit, find your True Essence."

Tikki smiled at the mention of his favorite author. "But Thoreau did some of that in Maine."

Early shrugged. "Maybe she's an aspiring Hobbit and she needed bigger trees."

Tikki collapsed into laughter. He had already developed the typical Maine ironic humor, a useful tool for dealing with the pain of abandonment. He also thought that despite his father's profession, Early might never solve the mystery of why his marriage had collapsed.

Perhaps neither of them wanted to know why.

"You're cranky tonight because Mom is on your mind again?"

Early leaned forward and wrung his hands. "I just wish her explanation was less vague. What the hell is a True Essence?" Early couldn't shake a nagging suspicion that she had a hunky lumberjack stashed in her yurt. *Hell, for all I know, the guy's name is True Essence.*

Wind chimes tinkling outside inspired Tikki to turn on the radio. Music had hazards as well as pleasures, and right now the hazard was Toto's "I'll Be Over You" coming out of the speaker. The sweet, sad song made Early's heart sink. He and his wife had danced to it on their first date, but now his fond memories mixed with the cold reality of her abandonment. That song could have been written for him. *When will my heart stop breaking?*

The little black cat crawled from under the couch and jumped into the bay window. She yawned and stretched until it seemed like her bones would crack, and then sat observing her humans, wide yellow eyes making her look like an owl in a fur suit.

Early was glad for the distraction. "Sorry I scared you, kitty. Hey Tikki, are you ever gonna name that cat?"

Tikki shrugged. "I can't think of a good enough name. She's such an aristocat."

Early groaned, and then said, "She's the only female in the house right now. The Queen. Why don't you name her Queenie?"

"Borrrring."

"Mroww," the cat said, her gleaming black tail lashing back and forth.

"Should I have said Queen Latifah?" Early asked. The cat began to scratch, causing him to wonder if the fleas were this bad in Oregon. An image of his wife scratching in her yurt popped into his head and he burst out in a hearty, gut-shaking, mean-spirited giggle.

"I've been calling her Detective Cat," Tikki said, wondering why his father was laughing at the cat. "Or DC, but that might sound too political."

Early yawned and stretched like a giant black cat.

"Maybe I'm cranky because the case I'm taking on looks like it might only make me spin my wheels."

"Sounds like *Grand Theft Auto*."

"You play too many video games. There are no autos and no theft in this case. Chandler Hammond's sister wants me to find him."

"You mean that rich guy who took off with his girlfriend?"

Early's head flopped against the back of the couch. "Does the *Wall Street Journal* have a gossip column?"

"I hear things at school, you know." Tikki tugged on his ear.

"I didn't think what you heard at school concerned financiers."

"We don't always talk about girls, sports, and beer."

Tikki must be hanging out with some pretty boring kids. "His sister Honoria hasn't heard from him since he vanished, so she thinks something nefarious is up."

"Why? He skipped town with his girlfriend. Seems pretty straightforward to me."

"Me too." Early sighed. "That's the problem—there's not a chance in hell of finding Hammond if he wants to stay lost. But I can't say she's altogether wrong, because some things don't add up."

"Like what?"

"Like his ten-million-dollar company being dead in the water because nobody took over when he left."

Tikki whistled. "Hard to believe a ten-mil art business would be in Maine. Although these days, you sell one Van Gogh and you're rolling in dough."

"But Tikki, you have to already be rolling in dough to have a Van Gogh. Hammond raises capital from investors, but a company needs collateral to lure those investors. I can't imagine what he's using. The entire company seems to consist of just him."

"Stock certificates?"

Early snapped his fingers. "There's an idea—I'll issue stock for the Early Detection Agency. You can attend their annual meeting at their beautiful international headquarters in downtown Finderne."

"Dad, I'd rather not visit you in jail."

"Chandler Hammond isn't in jail."

"Maybe he is. Maybe he's just lucky. And despite all those criminal video games you think I'm playing, I have no idea how to make bail."

"Don't worry about it," Early said. "Any P.I. would consider only whether the money is good. And Honoria's money is *real* good."

"Sounds like a no-brainer to me."

But Early wondered how long Honoria would let the case go unresolved. If she didn't specify a time frame, if she was in for the long haul, wouldn't he be taking her money for nothing? And that would be like selling out.

Then he realized that you can't sell out if you have nothing to sell. And he had nothing but his soul.

I wouldn't sell that. But I might rent it out for a while.

5

IN WHICH EARLY DECIDES WHETHER TO CHASE HIS TAIL

Early's huge Caprice squeezed into the short and well-manicured driveway of Honoria Hammond's tidy white New England saltbox. He felt like Alice in Moneyland, but only because he knew who lived here. No casual passerby would suspect the owner of this modest place possessed a considerable fortune. Honoria probably liked it that way.

He pressed the doorbell and a frantic, deep barking began inside. A short middle-aged woman in a dowdy, well-worn cardigan opened the door. She looked about as wealthy as the house did.

"Ms. Hammond?" he asked. For all he knew, she was the maid; but approaching her like the Lady of the Manor reduced the risk of insult to her and possible injury to him.

She nodded. "I'm Honoria Hammond."

"I'm James Early of the Early Detection Agency. We spoke on the phone yesterday." He pulled out a small leather folder and handed it over.

She took the folder and scrutinized his credentials while

Early scrutinized her. *That's not quite the smile of a viper, but she does look like the python that swallowed the alligator.*

She returned the folder and shook all the fingers of his hand she could grasp. "Nice to meet you, Mr. Early. Please call me Honoria. Do come in." She stepped aside.

"Please call me Early," he shouted over the loud barks, peering down the hallway in apprehension.

"What are you waiting for?" Honoria demanded.

"Could you secure your dog?"

"What? Oh, the dog."

She punched a button beside the door. The barking stopped.

Early tilted his head. "What just happened?"

"I silenced the dog, as you asked." She pointed to the button on the wall.

He stared at the button, aghast. "What did you do? Electrocute him?"

For a moment she seemed shocked herself, then started laughing. "Oh, no, Early, *this* is my dog." She pressed the button and the barking resumed.

"An electronic dog," Early marveled. "Ain't technology grand?"

"Certainly is. No dog food, no vet bills, no poop."

Early melted into laughter. Her unexpected wisecrack had broken the ice. *I wonder if teenagers can be electronicated.*

Early followed her into the living room, which was dominated by a large portrait of a man resembling Mark Twain. He didn't even have to read the brass nameplate on the bottom of the frame to know it was McKinley Hammond. Early almost felt obligated to salute him.

"Please, sit down." Honoria seated herself on the sumptuous red leather couch. "Coffee?"

"I can never have too much."

She took a coffeepot from a silver tray on the table and poured two cups.

Early settled into a designer chair and whipped out his cell phone. Honoria made a face. "You're recording us with that thing?"

"I find video to be more accurate than taking notes." In his labor-intensive business, Early always tried to conserve energy. Especially his.

"If you must. But I want to state for the record that I look terrible on camera." Her fingers fluffed her short dark curls.

"I promise to bring my cosmetician and hairdresser next time."

"Fine. But only if they use top of the line products." Honoria was only half kidding.

Early took a sip of coffee and said, "This is delicious."

"Of course. I drink only imported, organic, fair-trade coffee."

"I see." He put down his cup as carefully as possible. "Let's get down to business. Do you think your brother met with foul play because of what happened to your father?"

Her eyes widened. "You know about that?"

"I read the case file at the police station."

She lowered her eyes and turned her face away. "I . . . I don't want to talk about it. Chandler and I were very young at the time. That incident traumatized us for the rest of our lives."

Early started to sympathize with her. "I'm sorry to hear that. Do you think your brother was kidnapped too?"

"I considered that, but wouldn't there at least be a ransom note or something by now? There have been no demands, nothing of the kind." Her eyes narrowed. "Unless his wife got a communication from the kidnappers and decided to ignore it."

Early stopped sympathizing. "Why would she ignore a ransom demand?"

"She would if she doesn't want him back. She'd have all his money without having to put up with him."

Not having met Mrs. Hammond, Early had no way of assessing the possibility. "But couldn't he have a reason for leaving?"

Honoria leaned back into the sofa. "None that I can think of. I suspected something was wrong when he didn't make his usual visit with my company dividend. I thought it might have been an oversight, but I still hadn't heard from him a week later. That's very unusual for someone as conscientious as my brother."

"So, you have investments with him."

"Just in his company, Crystalline."

"And you receive dividends every month?"

"Very punctually until Chandler disappeared."

"When did you receive your last dividend?"

"Well over a month ago. Chandler usually shows up with the cash on the first of each month." She shrugged and pushed her hair back.

A company issuing dividends in cash raised questions Early felt he needed to address. He would leave that for later. "Did you call him to ask why your dividend was late?"

"I did, but he didn't answer. I couldn't leave a message because his voice mailbox was full. Out of desperation, I called that bitch he's married to."

Another indication of how much she hated her brother's wife. Early hoped he would never be on the receiving end of Honoria's formidable animosity.

"That woman expected me to believe the preposterous idea that Chandler had run away with his girlfriend," she went on.

"Why is that idea preposterous?"

She waved her hand. "He and his girlfriend have been together for years. Why would they disappear now? Where would they go? It's absurd. Nobody cared what they did." She squirmed and pulled down the hem of the designer dress under her cashmere cardigan.

"What do *you* think happened to him?"

She leaned forward, stared into Early's eyes, and lowered her voice. "I think his wife found a way to get rid of him."

Early leaned forward, stared back, and lowered his voice. "You mean . . . homicide?"

She frowned and nodded, her gaze falling to the antique kilim rug.

Early scratched his nose. *She thinks Hammond's running off with his girlfriend is preposterous, but the idea that his wife murdered him is plausible?* He started to see why Hal had called this case a dog. If Early wanted Honoria as a client, he needed to find a way to convince her that he took her wild concerns more seriously than the police had. But did he?

He tried reasoning. "Why would his wife want him dead?"

"I think she was afraid that he *would* run off with his girlfriend and leave her destitute. On the other hand, if she killed him, she could keep all his money for herself."

"You watch those television shows, too, eh?"

"Excuse me?"

"Never mind. Did he have life insurance?"

"Probably."

"How about a will?"

"I don't know."

"If he didn't, his wife would most likely inherit the business."

She crossed her arms and frowned. "I imagine so."

Early turned to check his cell phone, recording on the table. "What about you? What would you inherit?"

He almost heard Honoria's jaw drop. "*What?*"

He whipped around, but she was already out of her chair, stomping to the front door. "Honoria, what are you—"

"Even if I did inherit his money, do you think I would murder him for it? How could you say such a thing?" She grasped the doorknob. "Get the hell out of my house."

He ran to the door and jammed his huge hand against it. "Honoria, it's my job to consider every angle."

"You don't have to consider that one," she hissed.

His eyebrows rose. "I wouldn't be much of a detective if I didn't."

"Are you? Much of one?" she spat. Suddenly, she started sobbing.

"Please, calm down," Early said, taking her arm to steer her back to the sofa.

"Don't tell me to calm down," she snarled, pulling her arm away and wiping her eyes on her sleeve.

I sure don't want her crying on my shoulder. She might bite me. "I apologize for upsetting you, but I need to pursue all possibilities—even the ones you don't want to think about."

She allowed him to lead her back into the living room where they retook their seats. She dabbed her eyes with a tissue, and then glared at him. "Where were we? Oh yes, you were asking whether I killed Chandler for his money."

"Unfortunately, I've dealt with enough guilty clients to know that I always have to ask." Early sighed.

"I'm sorry to hear that." Her tone was more conciliatory but still sarcastic. "Truth is, I really don't know what I'd inherit." She stared into space for a moment, and then tugged on the hem of her dress again.

Feeling this discussion was way premature if Hammond

was still alive, Early came up with another idea. "Your brother's girlfriend vanished at the same time. Do you think his wife killed her too?"

"I wouldn't be surprised." She folded her arms and stared out the window.

What a lurid imagination. She should write murder mysteries. "Homicide is a pretty serious charge. Do you have any supporting evidence?"

"No. You're the evidence collector, you and the police." She picked up her coffee cup and stared into the steaming liquid. "I'd rather not have any evidence. I'd rather believe Chandler is alive. But I have this . . . feeling." She swirled her coffee. "He's been out of contact for weeks. I can't imagine any reason why outside of foul play."

"You and he are close?"

"Yes. I mean we used to be. We talked frequently." She put down her cup and picked at the plush piping on the couch.

"He never mentioned any plans to go away? Wishful-thinking stuff? Like the way Mainers talk about Florida during a long winter."

"Not that I recall." Her brows knit. "But he goes on many business trips, so I may not have noticed if he had talked about something like that."

"Do you remember your last conversation?"

"I believe we discussed a lobster festival he planned to attend on the midcoast this summer."

"Then he was thinking ahead. It doesn't sound like he was considering an imminent departure."

"One more reason why his sudden disappearance doesn't make sense." She clasped her hands around one knee and twisted to face the imposing portrait on the wall behind her. "Daddy, I'm sorry. I should have kept a closer eye on him. After your kidnapping, I never should have let him out of my sight." Her lower lip trembled and tears filled her eyes again. "Oh, Early, if anything has happened to Chandler—"

"Easy, Honoria." Early patted her shoulder as she wiped her face with a tissue. "We'll get to the bottom of this."

Oh hell, what did I just say? He had accepted the case. He couldn't unring that bell now. But she was right—her brother's disappearance was starting to stink worse than week-old lobster bait. "When did you have that conversation?"

"Maybe a week before he disappeared. I'll have to check my phone records. Maybe his wife knows what day he vanished. Especially if it was her idea."

She's quite reliable—mention his wife and she goes up like a rocket. He shifted in anticipation of her reaction to his next question. Guns, knives, and fists were no problem, but some of the questions he had to ask clients made him squirm.

"Have you ever met your brother's girlfriend?"

Much to his relief, she did not go ballistic. Maybe she liked his girlfriend more than his wife. "Taziz? Not in person."

He was surprised she knew the woman's name. He couldn't remember the names of *his* brother's girlfriends.

"I've seen her picture. She was one of Chandler's suppliers. He bought Middle East antiquities from her family and resold them through Crystalline. Apparently, they were well connected in Iraq, but Chandler never went into detail about that."

She invested in her brother's company but doesn't have much interest in its products, its business practices, or its financials. She's cool as long as the dividends keep coming.

Questioning her about Crystalline seemed futile, but he

had to try. "Did Chandler ever talk about Crystalline's finances? Or mention any money problems?"

"The only problem I recall arose when Saddam was deposed. Taziz and her family needed to escape the country quickly and that was the end of Chandler's trade in Iraq. The family hid out in France until Obama was elected, and then a friend of the President helped Chandler get Taziz into the U.S. I guess he was ready for a little fling." She sighed. "He always did have an eye for beautiful women."

"His business had some unexpected perks, eh?"

"Oh, I don't condemn him for cheating on his wife. I wonder why it didn't happen sooner. But I know very little about Crystalline except what I told you on the phone yesterday, that the company was worth ten million dollars."

Maine had a robust art scene, but Early still couldn't figure out why a multi-million-dollar art company, which could have headquartered anywhere, was operating out of a small-town basement. He was as suspicious as Honoria, but about different things and for different reasons. Was Hammond stealing Picassos? Maine's remote location offered good hiding places.

He came back to the financials. "Do you know anything about Crystalline's other investors?"

"No. I don't scrutinize my brother's business dealings over his shoulder. Although I'm sure his wife pays plenty of attention to the money, since she's very fond of spending it." She snorted.

"Many women who are fond of spending their husbands' money couldn't care less about where it comes from. Mob wives, for instance."

"He had no mob association. And I'm sure that little bitch doesn't hesitate to poke her expensively sculpted nose into his business affairs." She sniffed. "I'll bet she even prowls through his things when he's gone. She'd probably be a gold mine of information for you." She waved her finger in his face.

Early was bemused by Honoria's intense loathing. "Why do you hate your brother's wife?"

"I'm ashamed to admit she was a trashy little dancer he picked up in one of those so-called gentlemen's clubs. She knew a meal ticket when she saw one and set her sights right on him. That greedy bitch doesn't love him; she's just after his money."

Considering how important money was to Honoria, her statement didn't surprise Early. "Do you have any idea where your brother could be? Maybe a favorite vacation spot?"

"Vacation? What's that? He works all the time. The only trips he takes are for business."

"Is there any particular place where he does a lot of business?"

"Yes. His office."

Early grimaced. The woman was mercurial—first outraged, then mourning, now toying with him. "I mean does he travel to one location more frequently than others?"

"Sorry. He goes to Boston a great deal. Maybe he likes the Red Sox." She snickered. "He told me he has a college friend there, a real estate agent named Larry Bloch."

"Does his girlfriend go with him?"

"I wouldn't be surprised. His trips can last more than a week, sometimes to nice places like the Caribbean in winter. I imagine he'd be in no hurry to come home if he's with Taziz."

"Does he call you when he's on a trip?"

"At least once, if only to check in."

"Can you tell me anything else about his girlfriend?"

"Not really. He doesn't talk about her much."

"Ever seen any of the artifacts he sells?"

She paused. "Now that you mention it, I don't think I have. But not being a collector, I doubt I'd know an artifact if I fell over one."

Early thought her falling over one was unlikely. He tried a different approach. "Could his girlfriend have done away with him, not his wife?"

Honoria pursed her lips. Early could tell she liked the wife idea better.

Finally, she said, "I don't know why Taziz would do such a thing. A woman in her situation . . . what motive would she have? Chandler was making money for her and when that dried up, he got her into this country. Why murder him?"

"Maybe he left her a big chunk of change in his purported will. Maybe he was going to dump her and go back to his wife." Early had discovered how to stick it right back to Honoria.

"Those are unknown factors."

"But they make sense," he said, knowing sense wasn't always pertinent. "So, nothing comes to mind when you consider where he could be?"

Her eyes widened. "Maybe the family camp? I don't know why he would go up there before summer starts, but there's no cell phone signal. That could explain why he hasn't called."

"Pretty remote, eh? I'd like to take a look."

"You'll agree to help me?"

He still felt the case wasn't quite cohesive, but Honoria's overwhelming conviction gave him a slight surge of confidence. Maybe he could do this. There was only one way to find out. "Yeah, I'll take your case." He held out his hand and hers disappeared into it as they shook.

"Thank you," she said. "I knew you would see things my way."

He ignored her presumptuous remark. "Do you have a map to the family camp?"

"No, but I can draw one."

That sounded like a losing proposition. "My car has GPS. Do you know the coordinates?"

Honoria giggled. "In Maine, you're lucky to get directions. And you know what they would sound like: 'Go a fair piece down the road, deah, to wheah the pink church usta be.'"

He had to laugh. Even now there are places in Maine where you can't get theah from heah. "Draw me a map, then. How are you at figuring mileage?"

"Don't know, I've never tried."

He was already starting to regret his decision. Getting lost in the Maine woods wasn't hard—people wandering a few hundred feet off a trail have been known to become lost for days. But he would never find the place without her help, as vague as that might be. Maine camps were way off the grid for good reason, some accessible only by boat.

Honoria scrawled on a notepad, labels and arrows running in every direction. "Here's the logging road. A few miles up on the right is the driveway, which goes uphill about a mile. At the end"—she drew a square topped by a triangle to designate the cabin—"there's propane appliances and heat. We don't go up to camp in the winter but summer nights can get pretty chilly."

"Who else uses the place?"

"Myself, Chandler, his wife."

"His girlfriend?"

"Probably. I don't doubt they have a high old time up there now and then."

"Does your brother hunt or fish? Ski, snowshoe, sled?"

"No, he's not much of a sportsman."

"Does he bring friends or clients up there for outings?"

"I don't think so. We usually go for the solitude."

Early dreaded the one question left to ask. "Honoria . . ."

Apparently, she had learned his approach. "Another tough question? Let's have it." She clenched her jaw and raised her chin.

"Any possibility of . . . drugs?"

"Absolutely not. I've never seen Chandler so much as smoke a cigarette."

He tilted his head. "You're sure? Sometimes we don't know people as well as we think."

She ran her fingernail along the sofa's plush piping again, and then looked off to the side and said, "You're right. But I've never seen my brother with drugs; he's never mentioned drugs; and as far as I can tell, I've never seen him under the influence of drugs. So, I'll say no and hope that's the truth. I can't swear on our mother's grave that he never got involved in anything unsavory. If he did, I hate to think about what could have happened . . ." Her voice trailed off.

Early had seen some of the ugly scenarios she hated to think about. "You're probably right. I've seen no signs of drug involvement." He hoped his lame consolation reassured her—thus far he hadn't seen much of anything.

She smiled and pulled a fat red leather checkbook and a Cross pen from a gold-inlaid box on the table. "What's your retainer?"

Early smiled back. Her case might turn out to be a dog, but this part was his idea of Best in Show.

6

IN WHICH EARLY FINDS THAT WHERE
THERE'S SMOKE, THERE'S MORE SMOKE

Because the massive iron driveway gate was open, Early didn't need to use the call box or his car as a battering ram. The name *Hammond* carved into a huge rock beside the driveway confirmed this was the right place. Rocks in Maine are usually free but someone had spent a few bucks on that one.

Huge old-growth pine trees and expensive landscaping lined a gracious winding driveway that was big enough for his car. This place was a sharp contrast to Honoria's modest home. He figured just keeping the lawn mowed must cost a fortune.

He drove around the next curve to see a large mansion in traditional Maine gray. Clouds of smoke the same color emanated from behind it.

Early jammed on the brakes, grabbed his fire extinguisher, and hit the ground running. "Fire. Is anybody home? Fire!"

The house's huge size obscured the origin of the fire. Taking his best guess, he ran into the smoke where he barely discerned the shimmering figure of a woman waving a newspaper. He thought she was trying to disperse the smoke, but he realized she was fanning a blazing trash can. *What the hell?*

Early whirled around for a gulp of fresh air. He held his breath and plunged through the smoke to grab the woman's arm.

"Ow!" she wailed, dropping the newspaper and spinning to kick and punch him. "Who the hell are you? Let me go, you son of a bitch."

"What are you doing?" His efforts to avoid her flying fists and feet were futile. "Ouch! Why are you torching the place?"

"Am not," she hollered, wrenching her arm free. She turned to run but Early pounced on her, pinning her to the ground. She pulled out her cell phone, punched a button, and screamed, "Assault," before resuming her flailing.

"Stop it or I'll slap the cuffs on you," he bellowed, trying to dodge the blows.

"Get the hell off me you bastard. Help! *Help!*" She twisted around and smacked her foot upside his head. Knocked off balance, he did an inglorious face plant into the grass while she scrambled to her feet and ran back to the trash can.

Early propped himself up on one elbow and rubbed his throbbing ear. *Damn, I need to work out more.*

The fire was more important than this maniacal woman. He seized his fire extinguisher and sought the source of the flames, but his watering eyes and choking throat hampered his efforts. He waved his arms to clear the smoke with little success.

Bent over wheezing, he heard a distant siren. A hazy flash of red lights was coming up the driveway. *Firefighters.*

Suddenly, he was pushed to the ground. His fire extinguisher went flying and he felt the cold hard slap of handcuffs around his wrists. A police officer pulled him to his feet and shoved him toward a cruiser in the driveway. "You have the right to remain silent—"

Early stumbled a few steps, planted his feet, and twisted around, his nose inches from the cop's face. "Hi, Jeremy."

The stunned officer brushed aside a clump of red hair along with smoky tears. "Early? What in the hell are you doing here?"

"I *thought* I was collaring an arsonist. See the smoke?" He tried to point with his manacled hands, but he wasn't a contortionist.

Jeremy looked from Early to the smoke and back. "Dispatch reported an assault at the Hammond estate and I was the nearest unit."

"An assault? Yeah, on me."

"You were assaulted? What happened?"

"I have an appointment to interview Mrs. Hammond about her husband's disappearance."

"Oh yeah, Chandler Hammond. Didn't he run off with his girlfriend?"

Early sighed. "Whatever. I saw the smoke when I arrived and grabbed my fire extinguisher—see it lying over there? I entered the backyard and observed a woman fanning a fire in a trash can over yonder. I interpreted this as arson and attempted to apprehend her."

Jeremy shook his head. "Only you could come up with a story like that."

"It's true. Is that Hammond's wife over there? We haven't been properly introduced yet."

The wind had shifted and blown most of the smoke away. Jeremy glanced at the woman, now visible and still fanning the fire in yonder trash can. "Yeah, that's Siri Hammond. Did she assault you?"

"Damn skippy. Ask her about our appointment if you don't believe me."

"I didn't say I don't believe you. What I can't believe is the way you always seem to run into trouble."

"Trouble is my business," Early said, relishing the rare opportunity to play hardboiled detective. His Lieutenant Columbo trench coat wasn't his only affectation.

"Wicked pissah. Who called 911?"

"She must have done it when she pulled out her cell phone."

The cop's jaw dropped. "While she was assaulting you?"

"I think at that point we were assaulting each other."

Jeremy flashed an evil grin. "Are you confessing?"

"Hell no."

"Sounds like it. Now let me get this straight: you tried to arrest her for arson, she called in an assault, and this whole situation is a misunderstanding."

"That's right. It's probably the usual—this being Maine, she wasn't expecting a black guy to show up."

Early was never considered a suspicious person because the police chief was his best friend. But he couldn't avoid Jeremy's ribbing. "Especially one as big and mean-looking as you. Why not try shucking and jiving? You might have scared her less."

"Shucking and jiving? How quaint. And I don't think shucking and jiving during a fire is such a hot idea, so to speak."

"Argh. Come on, ya nummy." Jeremy grabbed his arm and dragged him over to Siri. "Mrs. Hammond, this man says he has an appointment with you this afternoon."

A confused Siri glanced back and forth between them. Early figured he'd better speak up.

"Mrs. Hammond, I'm James Early of the Early Detection Agency. I called yesterday about interviewing you regarding the disappearance of your husband." He almost expected her to say: oh yeah, the rich guy who took off with his girl-friend. "We agreed to meet here this afternoon."

He was thankful to see the dawn rise in her big brown eyes. "*You,*" she nearly squeaked, "are Mr. Early? I am very sorry." She grabbed his arm and looked at Jeremy. "That's right, officer, we do have a meeting this afternoon."

Early glared at Jeremy and wiggled his handcuffed wrists. Jeremy freed him.

"I'm sorry for the rough treatment and the mix-up, Mrs. Hammond," Early said, rubbing his wrists, "but I believed I was witnessing an arson."

"I appreciate your concern, Mr. Early." Siri laughed. "But this isn't arson. I'm just making pottery."

Early glanced around. The chaotic scene looked like the kind of activity his son would love.

"If we're straightened out, I'll go report in at the station," Jeremy said.

Siri nodded and turned her attention to the trash can.

Passing Early on the way to his cruiser, Jeremy smirked and said, "Need any assistance fighting off the women? Or can you handle things with your teeny little equipment?"

"If I ever start fighting off women, I'll need more help than just you."

"Duly noted, sport." Jeremy saluted and got into the car.

A sudden thought sent Early running toward the cruiser. "Jeremy, wait!"

Jeremy unlocked the passenger door to let Early slide in. "What's on your so-called mind Early?"

"Knock it off, you insufferable twit. You live close to here don't you?"

"About a half mile down the road. You gonna drop in? I'm not anticipating any fires."

Early rolled his eyes. "Forget the fire. When was the last time you saw Chandler Hammond?"

Jeremy leaned back and stared at the headliner. "Well, even though we're nearly neighbors by country standards, we didn't exactly chat over the backyard fence."

"No surprise. Apparently, the country club and Chamber of Commerce meetings are the only socializing he ever does. And that's just to pull in more investors."

"He seems like quite the money shark." Jeremy pondered the question for another moment. "I'd say I last saw him about a month ago."

"Around the time of his disappearance?"

"Yeah. Late at night or more like early morning. I was on my way home after coming off shift when I saw his car pulling out of here." He gestured toward the end of the driveway.

"Which way was he headed?" Early asked.

"Away from town. And in one hell of a hurry—he tore outta here like his ass was on fire and he had no teeny little extinguisher."

"Can we bypass your cute wisecracks?"

"Aw, Early, I didn't know you thought I was cute." Jeremy batted his eyelashes.

"Cut that shit out. There's enough room in here to give you a good larruping."

"Assault on an officer? Where did I put those handcuffs?"

"Police brutality. I'm covered with bruises," Early said.

"From Siri."

"Who'd believe that?" Early chuckled.

Jeremy had no comeback. "You win. You think the night I saw him was the same night he ran off with his girlfriend?"

"If they did. You never saw him after that?"

"No, but I'm not exactly the neighborhood watchdog."

"Some cop," Early said.

"There's such a thing as off duty."

"Of course. I'd better get back to Siri before she forgets who the hell I am."

"Could be a valid concern. Later, dude," Jeremy said.

Early walked back to see Siri putting a cover on the smoking trash can. "Mr. Early, I really am sorry about this." She seemed to be getting pretty good at the apology thing.

"At least we cleared things up. Just what *is* going on here?"

Siri smiled, walked to another trash can, lifted the lid, and liberated a huge smoke cloud, causing Early to duck. She grabbed some tongs, pulled a smoking ash-covered pot from the can, and ran to dunk it in the nearby swimming pool. Early watched as the smoke turned into steam. She retrieved the pot, dumped the water out, placed it on the patio beside the pool, and walked back to Early.

"This process is called raku," she said. "It's an ancient Asian technique of pottery making and my specialty. Perhaps you're familiar with my art studio, Siri's Seramics? My work is displayed in finer galleries and shops all over the world."

Early had never heard of her studio or of raku. But to soften her up for questioning he tried to look as impressed with her pots as she was with herself. It was no easy task. "You make your pottery in this shed?"

"Yes, my wheel and kiln are inside. Come on." Inside the shed was a floor-to-ceiling kiln as well as several rows of tables holding many finished pots. On the far side of the room, several people were rolling pots in bubble wrap and packing them into large straw-filled wooden crates.

"We're shipping this batch to an exhibit in California," Siri boasted. "It's the biggest invitational gathering on the west coast. We'll be out there for about a week."

Early didn't have to fake his wonder as he gazed at the pottery. The beautiful red glaze on her pots was the most striking color he had ever seen. His genuine appreciation made discussing her pottery, and thus gaining her confidence, even easier. "How do you produce those vivid colors?"

Siri chuckled, pleased to showcase her artistic talents before this new admirer. "When I fire the pots, I place different additives into the kiln with them to see their effects on the glaze. The process I'm using today is called Saggar firing. I wrap the additives in aluminum foil before I put them into the kiln. Additives can consist of many different things: marbles, horsehair, manure, metal dust. I like to experiment with unusual ideas. I'm only limited by my imagination."

"Your imagination has great results. Those pots are stunning." He picked up a large tawny vase and examined its graceful swirl design, running his fingers over the cool smooth surface. "That looks like a feather?"

Siri grinned widely. "Yes, an emu feather. When feathers hit a hot pot, they vaporize and leave that kind of design. It's called feather pottery. On that pot I used a slip called terra sigillata. Terra sigillata gives the pottery a buttery feel."

The mention of butter made Early want to drool. He quickly returned the pot to the table.

Siri rambled on. "There's no glaze at all on that pot. I buff the greenware—that's an unfired pot."

Early appreciated the explanation since he could see the pot wasn't green.

"I buff the pot with dry cleaner bags, brush on the slip, and then fire the pot and apply the feather to the hot pot. After the feather vaporizes and the pot cools, I wash it and let it dry for a couple of days. When the pot is ready, I sand off the rough edges and apply up to ten coats of floor wax, buffing between each coat. And then, *wah-lah*, the pot is done."

"Sounds like a lot of work," Early said.

"That's why art pottery is valuable and expensive."

"I'd say pots like these are worth the price."

He noticed his own professional technique was having the desired effect—she beamed at him like he was her new best friend. "Thank you, Mr. Early. I'd like to use turkey feathers, but they're hard to find. It seems the birds like to keep their feathers on."

Early envisioned an ugly flock of naked turkeys. "I hope so. Looks like you can make a lot of pots in a kiln that size."

"My kiln can handle up to several dozen pots depending on how big they are."

Early wondered whether her art was profitable or a money pit. Sometimes details that seemed unrelated or unimportant during a case turned out to be the opposite. "Your kiln must be expensive to run."

"It is but my pots often sell for thousands of dollars." She sniffed. "I was telling you about raku: while the pots fire in the kiln, I fill these trash cans with straw or newspaper. The *New York Times* is best, they use great ink. When I place the hot pots in the trash cans, they set the newspaper or straw on fire. Then I 'burp' the cans—remove the lid to let in more air, which flares up the fire. That produces a lot of smoke." She laughed. "So, you see there is a fire, but only in the trash cans."

"And then?"

"Timing is a judgment call. When the pots are finished smoking, I pull them out of the cans and dunk them into water. That's why my kiln is close to the swimming pool. The cool water makes the colors really pop."

"Doesn't that dirty up the pool?"

"We never swim in it anyway. Chandler always hated the pool."

Hated, not hates? Interesting.

Early wondered how Siri would feel about her pottery if it didn't sell. What sounded cynical he preferred to call critical thinking. "And you sell your finished pottery through your husband's company, the Crystalline Art Distributorship?"

He was surprised to see her frown. "Yes, Crystalline does distribute my work." Apparently, she was passionate about her pottery but not about her husband and his company. "Why don't we get to our meeting. These people don't need my help and there are no more pots ready for dunking right now."

Early followed her up the winding Belgian block walkway to the mansion, hoping to find out what was lurking behind her strange reaction to his last question.

7

IN WHICH EARLY GETS ICED

Early walked into a kitchen so cavernous he expected to see bats hanging from the ceiling, but it was more like a crystal cave with clear glass shelves in place of cabinets. They gave the room an ice-palace look—perfect for Siri.

He tossed his trench coat onto a spotless gleaming chair. Siri made a face, but Early didn't notice. He was remembering the warm and cozy farmhouse kitchen of his South Jersey childhood. He could almost smell the coffee his mother kept warm on the back of their caramel-colored woodstove. It was worlds away from where he now sat at a clear glass table.

"Coffee?" Siri asked.

"Please. Black, no sugar."

She fussed over an electric kettle on the black granite counter; then, she slapped a cup of instant coffee in front of him and sat down. "Honoria is still in a snit, huh?"

How does she know that? "I can't reveal my client."

"You don't have to." Siri's gaze fluttered up to the ten-foot ceiling. "I know this investigation is her idea." She leaned toward Early. "Honoria doesn't like to think her sainted brother is a mere mortal who would do something like running off with his girlfriend. But I'm not going to disguise the truth just to make that bitch happy."

This answered another question—Siri bore scorching enmity toward Honoria. Since she would be reluctant to help him if she thought he was Honoria's hired gun, he tried to establish a neutral position.

"Honoria's entitled to her opinion," he said. "It's my job to be thorough and ask the routine questions. I know you made a statement to the police and I appreciate your cooperation."

He placed his cell phone on the table and began recording. Siri objected but not quite in the same way Honoria had. "Just a moment."

She dashed to the counter to grab a large makeup mirror and a box; then, she returned to the table and opened the box. Early glimpsed a huge assortment of makeup items with unpronounceable names.

He gulped down some much-needed coffee and said, "When was the last time you saw your husband?"

Siri positioned the mirror in front of her face, pulled a brush from the box, and perused several pots of powder before choosing one. "A few weeks ago, I think." She swirled powder onto the brush and then onto her face. "We went to bed and when I woke up the next day he wasn't around." She waved the brush in the air, dropping powder onto the pristine table. "He spends every morning in his office; then, he stops for lunch."

"He works at home all day?"

"Except when he's away on business." She finished dusting her face and picked up a tube of very shiny bright red lipstick. "His routine is pretty reliable; when I didn't see him in the kitchen at lunchtime, I checked his office. He wasn't there, either."

"Could he have gone on a business trip and forgotten to tell you?"

"Hardly." She applied the lipstick, smacked her very shiny bright red lips, and blotted them with a paper towel. "Chandler travels a lot but always gives me his itinerary: when he's leaving, where he's going, who he's meeting, how long he'll be gone. In case something comes up." She traded the lipstick for a different brush and began plastering her long lashes with jet black mascara.

"So, he didn't leave any word about where he'd be that day."

"No. I thought he might have gone up to his family's mountain camp. I looked for a note but didn't find one. I even checked my cell phone but there were no new text messages or voice mails from him.

"Then, I realized his laptop was missing. He doesn't take it up there with him because there is no internet access. I wondered if we'd had a burglary during the night and the alarm had malfunctioned. I checked the safe and found it was empty."

"What do you usually keep in the safe?"

"I don't keep anything in it. Chandler keeps the company files, maybe some money . . ."

"Everything was missing?"

"Nothing was in the safe. I didn't think anyone would steal his company files. Then, a very bad feeling came over me." She dropped the mascara and grabbed a tin of blusher. "I called Chandler's cell phone. It went directly to voicemail and I left a message. But when I couldn't shake my apprehension, I called Taziz's cell phone."

Early was surprised that Siri would call her husband's girlfriend. "What did she say?"

"Her phone went right to voicemail too, and her message said she was out of the country."

Early still hadn't heard anything to contradict that Hammond had run off with his girlfriend. "Did you call the police to say you might have been burglarized?"

She dipped a sponge into the tin of blusher, rubbed ruddy circles on her cheeks, and turned to check all angles in the mirror. "No."

Early tilted his head. "Why not?"

She put down the sponge and sighed. "My bad feeling wasn't about a burglary. My husband, his computer, and the contents of his safe were all gone. He wasn't answering his phone, he left no information on where he would be, and his girlfriend was out of the country. Wouldn't you draw the obvious conclusion?"

"I'd say everybody has."

"Everybody but Honoria." Siri tapped her long and richly-enameled fingernails on the tabletop, then yelled, "Dammit, I broke a nail." She grabbed a glass emery board from the box and began filing. "Shit, I'll need to have my entire manicure redone and I don't have time. It will just have to wait until I get to California."

The nail file's screeching put Early on edge. Was she trying to use the noise to distract him? He gritted his teeth. "Have you heard from him since then?"

She pouted, wrinkling her flawless skin. "No, but I don't expect to." She blew the dust off her nail and scrutinized her filing. "He's probably too busy playing hide the sausage with Taziz."

For once Early was glad he hadn't taken a sip of coffee. Spewing coffee all over Siri's perfect makeup and immaculate kitchen table would have been embarrassing. He managed to keep his game face on. "You don't seem upset about his disappearance."

She glared at him. "Of course, I'm upset—look at the mess he left me. I had to sell his car just to pay the staff. When the money's gone, they will be too."

She's upset about the financial mess, but she's not the broken-hearted person Amber saw in the cards. "Has anyone else heard from him? Investors in his company, colleagues at the Chamber of Commerce?"

"I don't know any of his investors. I've never met any Chamber members."

"Can we check his voicemail and text messages? Got his password?"

Siri snorted and returned to admiring her makeup in the mirror. "I'm lucky to have the safe combination. Chandler likes to hide things other than the sausage."

I wish she'd shut up about that sausage. Early rubbed his face. Maybe if he blindsided her. "Could Taziz have done away with him and taken off with the money?"

Something shook loose. Siri gasped and whirled to face him, knocking over his coffee cup. She looked at the spill in horror and then ran to fetch a paper towel.

Early replaced the cup in its saucer as Siri sopped up spilled coffee from the tabletop and highly polished black-and-white tile floor. "Oh hell," she moaned, "I'll have to find somebody to clean up this mess."

"Don't worry about that," Early said. "Here, sit down." He went to the counter, fixed some instant coffee, and handed it to her.

She took a sip, stared into the cup for a long time, and then murmured, "You're talking about . . . murder?"

"I have to consider all possibilities."

Her well-groomed eyebrows knit together as she raised her distressed eyes to his. "I—I don't think that's what happened, but . . . well . . . I suspect Taziz likes his money more than she likes him." She sat back, took a very deep breath, and exhaled.

Early thought Stevie Wonder could have seen through her act. Siri seemed indifferent to her husband's cheating. Honoria claimed Siri wanted Hammond's money, and Siri said Taziz wanted it. Early wondered why the guy had stuck around at all.

"Can you think of any reason for his sudden departure?"

She rolled her big brown eyes, sloshing her big brown coffee. "Chandler doesn't need reasons. He has these quirks."

Early sympathized—she could be describing his runaway wife. But his job was to be suspicious, not sympathetic. "So, you don't suspect foul play?"

"Chandler's too careful for something like that to happen to him. He's a very . . . *cautious* man," she almost sneered.

"Except when it comes to his girlfriend, eh? Everybody knows about her."

"Everybody knows she's a gold-digging bitch."

Listening to Siri echo Honoria, Early found it hard to suppress a laugh. Maybe Taziz said the same thing about both of them. *It would be a hoot to tell them they all call each other the same names. Or do they already know?*

"Chandler's smart about some things but not about women. He can't see his girlfriend is just kissing his ass. Or whatever she's kissing."

Ugh. More sausage talk. Early pressed on. "He's careful but not perceptive, eh?"

She seemed to laugh at a private joke. Early wondered if he'd find out what it was.

"Could he have been the victim of a scam gone bad?" he asked.

She put down her cup. "Seems unlikely. He's naïve about women, but not about his work. Once I asked him about some scams that were going around. He said his Chamber membership kept him on top of them and I can't imagine Chandler falling for one."

"Did you ever meet Taziz?"

She flipped a lock of long blonde hair over her shoulder. "Yes. She was around here more than I liked. Chandler says he has 'official' dealings with her due to her connections but those are gone. He's not fooling anybody now."

"I understand she was one of his suppliers."

"He bought artifacts from her family in Iraq until the regime change."

That agreed with Honoria's information. "Ever seen any of those artifacts?"

"No, but I wasn't involved in company dealings."

Too busy shopping, Early supposed. All the women in this family were concerned with either getting or spending money. "When was the last time you saw Taziz?"

"I never saw her again after Chandler vanished, which is why I figured she went with him. That was a few weeks ago."

Early disliked her vague timeline—he knew *exactly* when his wife had left. "Any indications that they planned to leave? Like passports or luggage lying around?"

"Not that I noticed."

"Could something around here help track him down? Files or correspondence?"

"We could check his office. I haven't touched anything but the safe."

Early grabbed his cell phone and followed her down the short hallway to the office. He swept his phone across the spacious and barren room, capturing every detail on video, including a nice view of the lush back garden through large French doors. *This makes my office look like a dog house.*

An enormous oak desk dominated the room. Early tried one of the drawers. Locked. "Got the key to this?"

Siri shrugged. "I can't find any of his keys. He probably took all of them. Bastard."

"Any idea what's in here?"

"From what I've seen: energy bars, pens and pencils, newsletters. Whatever."

Early wondered why Hammond would lock up such unimportant items. In his viewfinder he saw a gigantic old safe, almost as tall as he was, sitting against the back wall. "Impressive safe."

"Chandler said he got a good deal on it after the First National Bank failed."

"Can we take a look inside?"

"It's empty, like I told you."

"Humor me please." He flashed a big grin hoping it would be a ladykiller.

The grin worked. Siri frowned but walked over to the safe and spun the dial. Early figured he'd use that grin more often.

Siri heaved open the safe's massive door. "See? Nothing."

She started to close the door, but Early shot out an arm to block her. "What's that?" He pulled a small shiny object from the safe's solitary shelf.

"Oh, hehe." Siri's casual laugh was sounding a little less phony with practice. "I must have missed that. Looks like one of Chandler's flash drives."

"What's on it?"

"Probably family correspondence, photos, things like that."

"Can we take a look?"

"No."

His luck had run out. "Why not?"

"That stuff is . . . personal."

He pursed his lips. He hadn't figured her for the amateur porn type. But his grin had lost its magic and he gave in. "I think we're done in here for now. Can I see the basement?"

Siri hesitated. "Why?"

"Isn't that where your husband kept the inventory?"

She kept staring at him but did not respond.

"That's what I've been told," he said.

"He used to keep it there, but he hasn't had a new supplier since Taziz left Iraq. Everything in the basement was sold and shipped out long ago."

If there ever was anything down there. Somebody is hiding something. And Siri probably isn't going to stand for my forcing her to let me see something again after that smooth move I made on the safe. "Okay, let's go back to the kitchen and finish up this interview."

She closed the safe and they returned to the kitchen. Early relocated his cell phone on the icy table while Siri brought over two fresh cups of coffee.

"Was Crystalline your husband's only source of income?"

"He inherited a great deal of his money. He might have some investments too. I really don't know much about this finance stuff."

No surprise there. When it came to talking about finances Siri was trying to be as dry as the Desert of Maine. But Early wanted any information he could get about the company no matter how minuscule.

"Crystalline was the only business I've ever heard Chandler mention," she offered.

"What bank handled the company account?"

"I couldn't find an account. Not for him or the company. If they ever existed, he either closed them or hid them offshore using his financier tricks."

"Financiers never seem to run out of those tricks. If you're right, I doubt we'll ever find them."

Siri checked the makeup mirror again, pulled a tiny brush from the box, and began applying bright red lip liner. Early thought she might as well have been applying glue. Did she really think he was buying her claim of total ignorance?

The interview was giving him a headache. He wasn't hitting on all cylinders, which could be disastrous when dealing with a weasel like Siri. He decided to change tactics. "I'd like to talk to your staff members."

"Fine, but you'll have to wait. The regular staff has the week off. I'm going to pay them and then dismiss them when I come back from California. I don't know where they'll be after that."

"What about the pottery packers in the shed?"

"They're with the shipping company. It provides staff to handle large or fragile shipments."

"Does your regular staff live in the mansion?"

"No, although somebody might stay overnight if the snow gets too deep."

"You'll be in California for a week?"

"At least. I'm leaving as soon as the delivery truck is loaded this afternoon. I might be gone longer because I expect to be quite busy with orders. Oh, here comes the truck now." She stood and stared out the window at a huge

UPS truck coming up the driveway. "Are we done here, Mr. Early? I need to supervise the loading."

"For now, but I'd like to talk to you further when you return."

"Uh-huh." She whisked the cups away.

Siri had sounded phony during the interview, but she didn't seem to be outright lying. She had taken pains to appear cooperative and forthcoming by volunteering more information than he had asked for. Nevertheless, Early was curious about the flash drive in the safe. Her efforts to minimize its importance meant the drive held something she didn't want anybody to see and he was determined to find out what it was.

They parted in the driveway as she hustled to wave the UPS truck to the shed. Early planned to be quite busy too, but he certainly didn't want her to know with what.

8

IN WHICH EARLY FINDS SOMETHING
WAY COOL

Almost Memorial Day. After a long Maine winter, everyone heads out of town for the mountains or the nearest body of water, making it the perfect time for a break-in. Early stayed in town in order to steal Siri's mysterious flash drive. Her excuse had been absurd—nobody kept family photos in a locked safe regardless of how incriminating they were.

At dusk, he parked his Caprice behind the Hammond estate, hopped a towering stone wall, and pulled on rubber gloves. He had noted a lack of surveillance cameras on his visit and he knew there were no motion detectors—they'd be a waste of money where deer and coyotes ran through backyards. Siri had mentioned an alarm system, but he was sure it was only for the house. With occasional exceptions, deer and coyotes don't do break-ins.

The house loomed before him like a haunted old mansion in the near dark. Early crouched in the bushes to look for signs of life. Siri's word was unreliable; he needed to make sure nobody was around.

After a while he stood up to stretch, long arms reaching

toward the skinny last quarter of the moon. *The horns of the moon our ancestors called it.* Not the best cover for burglary but his order for a dark moon had been placed too late.

"*Treachery*." That was Amber's word. She probably never thought of him as the treacherous one, burglarizing the Hammond mansion like this. As for the Sneak Thief card, here was Early doing just what her reading had indicated. Coincidence? Maybe. But sometimes there was just no explanation for her uncanny accuracy.

He watched the house for another hour before he figured that anybody who was going to show up would be here by now. His private investigator training and a summer job at a locksmith's shop had given him the tools to neutralize simple home alarms; he slipped across the dark patio and disconnected the alarm's power supply. This time a summer job had been more useful than his education was —life could be ironic. Sucking in a deep breath he walked over to the French doors to Hammond's office and turned the knob.

The doors weren't locked.

A shudder shook him. Unlocked doors were common in Maine, but finance guys weren't usually this freewheeling— maybe with other peoples' money but certainly not with their own. Had Siri forgotten to lock up? Or did the Hammonds rely on that monster safe to keep their belongings, well, safe? Both of them seemed lackadaisical about security, but that made Early's black-bag job easier. He wasn't complaining.

He opened the door, slowly placed one large foot into the darkened room to test the floor and heard a creak.

"Damn," he whispered. One would think a guy with Hammond's money could keep his house in better shape. Maybe the burglar alarm didn't even work.

Fortunately, nobody was around to hear the noise. Early exhaled and stalked over to the huge, heavy safe. The words *First National Bank* gleamed gold on the door under the beam of his tiny flashlight.

The safe was too old for security measures like time locks. Early knew most people don't lock their safes or they write down the combination somewhere like on the edge of a desk drawer. But he had no need to search for the combination—his video had caught Siri's fingers as she dialed. Later, he had picked out the numbers by replaying the video in slow motion.

He spun the dial with the combination he had observed and the safe gave it up. He pulled the heavy door open and swept the light around the cavernous interior. It was darker than the inside of a pocket until a gleam at the back of the lone shelf caught his eye.

Siri had moved the flash drive. That wasn't a good sign—it could mean she had erased the files. He grabbed the drive and held it under his flashlight to reveal the letters CAD written on its side in magic marker.

Crystalline Art Distributorship. Pay dirt.

He slipped the drive into his pocket and swept the beam across the shelf again but came up empty. He walked over to the oak desk, pulled out a small screwdriver, jimmied the lock, and rifled through the drawers. At least Siri's word here was good: he found energy bars, pencils, paper, and other miscellaneous items. But no laptop.

He gave the safe a last going-over but the single shelf was as empty as a roadside beer bottle. He rapped his knuckles against the safe's back wall and heard the ring of solid steel. No concealed compartment there. He swept the light beam over the safe's floor, which was also barren, then dropped and crawled inside. At the very back, he found a sizeable object covered by a blanket. He pulled the blanket off to reveal a large cooler.

What the hell? In a case full of oddities here was another one. Why stash a cooler in a safe? Beer wasn't *that* expensive. Maybe Hammond was trying to keep the hired help from dipping into his pricey liquor but anybody living in a place like this could afford a liquor locker. Maybe Hammond liked *really* cold cash.

After much grunting, tugging, and cussing, Early had to admit the cooler was too heavy for him to move. Then he noticed a bit of clearance between the cooler and the shelf above it. He placed his flashlight into his mouth, raised the lid as far as he could, and slid his hand inside. Something under his fingers felt smooth and cold. An ice slab? *Imagine that, ice in a cooler.*

He tried grasping the cold object. It was too slippery, but drying his gloved hand on his shirt gave him enough traction to raise it. He slid his hand underneath and heard the crackling sound of a plastic bag. He squeezed. What he felt was long and lumpy like a . . . finger? Something hard seemed to encircle it. Something in the shape of a ring—

A loud click startled him. Somebody was unlocking the front door.

Frozen fingers fumbling, Early dropped the lid. He replaced the blanket, quietly closed the safe door, and spun the dial. Then he leaped toward the French doors like a big black panther, hoping to avoid the creaky floorboards. He softly closed the door as he slipped outside, jumped into the bushes, and squatted.

The office light blazed on, temporarily blinding him. His eyes recovered to see a beautiful woman walking into the room. Early flattened his body against the cold ground and peered under the bushes while trying to slow his breathing.

She didn't look familiar. He would never forget a woman with flowing waist-length black hair and a bodacious rack like hers. Early didn't go for the unblack type, but she appeared to be more bronze than white.

Was she one of the staff returning from vacation ahead of time? He shook his head. She didn't look like the hired help.

She glanced around the room, crossed to the middle, and began pulling up the rug. Puzzled and curious, Early stood up for a better view.

She was opening the door of a safe hidden in the floor.

Now he realized why Hammond's safe was empty. The big safe was a ringer and the *real* goodies were in that floor safe. Genius. The huge safe dominated the room, ensuring no one would suspect a second safe was concealed in the room. But this mysterious woman not only knew of its existence, she knew exactly where it was . . . and even the combination.

A hidden safe was a good way to let the Hammonds evade official inquiries. But if Siri didn't want anyone snooping into her activities, why didn't she keep the flash drive in the floor safe? Was she just careless?

Then a light clicked on in his brain: Siri wasn't hiding the flash drive, she was hiding whatever was in the cooler. The flash drive might have gotten into the safe by accident.

He had to find out what was inside that cooler. He needed to see—

Uh-oh, I think she just made me.

Maybe he had rustled the bushes or some critter had made a noise by running through the yard. Whatever the cause, the woman abruptly looked up, pulled a 9mm Glock pistol from her pocket, and pointed it right at his hiding place as she stalked toward the French doors.

Early didn't stop to determine the exact make of the pistol. His first thought was, *Jump back, Jack!* and he did just that. Hoping the moonlight was too dim for a lucky shot, he dashed across the backyard and cleared the stone wall like an Olympic hurdler. Better his back should kill him in the morning than she should kill him tonight.

He jumped into his car and waited for the trembling to stop. Burglary was nerve-wracking enough without facing down a gun.

When he regained enough composure to drive, he took the back roads home. The Finderne cops wouldn't think twice if they saw him roaming around at this hour, but he didn't want to be seen near a mansion that had just been burglarized. That could be a different story and he didn't think he'd like the ending.

Besides, the leisurely drive home gave him lots of time to think about why the hell somebody would lock a cooler inside a safe.

9

IN WHICH EARLY DISCOVERS HOW
HAMMOND MADE OFF

Early tossed the stolen flash drive onto the computer desk and sat down next to his son. "Check this out, Tikki. Let's see what kind of education you're getting."

"Sure." Tikki plugged the drive into a laptop port and whipped another drive out of the desk.

"What's that?" Early asked.

"A forensic program called COFEE. The cops use it to find evidence on confiscated computers."

Early stared at his kid for a long moment. "And may I ask how you acquired such specialized knowledge of forensic technology, Tikkitin?"

"From those damn video games, Dad."

"Watch your mouth young man. I mean where'd you get that program?"

Tikki grinned. "From Uncle Hal."

"You had a COFEE klatsch with him, eh?"

Tikki tilted his head. "What's a klatsch?"

"Never mind." He was relieved that Tikki hadn't downloaded something crazy, which avoided not only legal complications but huge computer repair bills.

"I'm just following in the great big footsteps of my Dad," Tikki said with a smirk.

Early blushed deep purple.

"What are you looking for on here?" Tikki asked.

"I believe that drive holds the financial records of the Crystalline Art Distributorship. Sudden disappearances like Hammond's can be red flags for financial misappropriation. I want you to find all the corporate accounting data you can, and then run the numbers to see if everything checks out."

"Cool. I love to run numbers."

Tikki's such a weird kid. And I wouldn't have it any other way.

The boy hit a few keys. "Here's a list of the files." He scrolled down the screen.

Early leaned forward in excitement, but his heart sank when he saw the files had titles like "Circus Tickets" and "Company Picnic." Maybe Siri was right—the drive contained family photos and letters. But if so, why was CAD written on it? Was that her opinion of Hammond?

Even personal documents can give up useful information. Early ignored his disappointment. "Let's open that first file."

"Okay. 'Circus Tickets.'" Tikki opened the file. "Looks like we won't need the COFEE program. This is just a spreadsheet of names and figures."

Early caught the name *Honoria Hammond* next to the number 50,000 on one line. "This could be Crystalline's investor list. Those numbers might be the amount each one invested. Doesn't seem like enough here to amount to ten million, though. Most seem to have under fifty thousand invested," Early said.

He scanned the names. They were like a who's who of

local business owners, politicians, officials, and other luminaries. But clearly the spreadsheet had no connection with circus tickets unless those people were buying the circus.

"Isn't expensive art usually sold at high-end auctions?" Early said.

"Yeah, from what I see in the business news," Tikki said.

"Most expensive artwork is in museums or private collections because regional galleries don't have the money to purchase them. How can Crystalline be worth millions of dollars like Hammond says?" Early turned to his son. "What do you think, Tikki? You must know about such things from reading the *Wall Street Journal*."

"Nah, I just look at the pictures. I'm the anti-*Playboy*."

Early burst out laughing. "Where do you get these ideas?"

"I just reversed what you told Mom the night she found those magazines stashed in the back of your closet."

"Ah . . . you remember that?" Early cleared his throat. "What was I saying?"

"You don't know how Crystalline could be worth millions of dollars."

"Oh, yeah. I don't think the *Wall Street Journal* would be interested in the Maine art scene but Crystalline should have gotten a mention in our local newspaper. They like to publicize thriving companies. It makes Maine look prosperous."

"Maybe Mr. Hammond isn't doing any deals."

"He has to, if he's conducting business."

"Maybe he's not conducting business."

Early raised his eyebrows. "Maybe we'll find out."

They continued down the list. "Wait a minute." Tikki cried. "Take a look at this last entry marked 'Larry.' There are seven entries by his name—each one for $125,000. He alone brings up Crystalline's bottom line considerably."

"Whoa!" said Early. "Could that be Larry Bloch, his college friend in Boston who Honoria mentioned? I think I need to talk to him. Look him up."

Tikki opened the browser and searched for several minutes.

"What's taking so long?" Early asked.

"I can't find anyone by that name in Boston."

"Did you try 'Lawrence'?"

Tikki rolled his eyes. "Dad, I've been searching the internet all my life. Of course I did."

"I'll search for him later. Keep looking through the rest of the files."

The rest of the names on the list belonged to members of the Chamber of Commerce or Hammond's country club. Early didn't move in those social circles.

"Some of these names on the list are the same as kids I go to school with," Tikki said.

Early rubbed his chin. Just how big a can of worms was he opening here?

Anxiety was making him hungry. He pulled on his trench coat. "I'm starving. Why don't I snag some Chinese from the restaurant downtown. Be back in a bit."

Early loaded up on Tikki's favorite Chinese delicacies and drove back home. The kid was working so hard, he deserved to be indulged. He walked in the door with his armful of food and said, "How's it going?"

"Oh, that smells so good it's making me drool," Tikki said. "I think I need some brain food because there's something I don't get. I'm no forensic accountant . . . yet. But according to these records, Siri's Seramics accounted for *all* of the company's sales. It's like Mr. Hammond was using the company as a tax write-off or something."

"No wonder Siri brags about her sales. She's got all his attention."

"I checked the company expenses, which were puny. Travel was the biggest followed by office supplies. But records of artwork he purchased? Zip. Nothing. He didn't purchase the artwork from his wife, so that wasn't an expense."

"What about the Iraqi artifacts Siri and Honoria said he bought?"

Tikki shook his head. "There are no records of them. Maybe he kept that information on another flash drive?"

"I scoured the safe. This drive was the only one there." *I don't think there was one in that cooler. Maybe Chandler took it with him? But then why did he leave this one behind?*

"I thought maybe he paid cash," Tikki said, "but there still should be a record of his transactions. I even checked the hidden files."

"Hidden files?" Early's head was spinning. "Great Hitchens' ghost. Besides avoiding taxes, I can think of only one reason to hide business files. Crystalline is starting to sound like a front."

"Money laundering, maybe? Kewl." Tikki grinned.

"Those damned video games," Early growled.

"I also found Mr. Hammond's sales-pitch letter. It says Crystalline offers investors a very generous twenty percent dividend. That's pretty good for a company with no profits, right? It also says their dividends will be automatically reinvested, not paid out to them. So, when you say Crystalline sounds like a front . . . this kind of data raises the Madoff flag."

"Bernard Madoff, who ran one of the longest-lasting

Ponzi schemes ever and is serving 150 years in the slammer for bilking thousands of people out of billions of dollars?"

"Yeah, him. The 'reinvestment' ploy is what let him hide his scam for so many years."

"That would put Hammond in some pretty rare company." Early shook his head. "But the Madoff story was all over the media. You don't think people could spot a scam now?"

"You've told me lots of times that greed trumps experience."

Early stared at the floor. "Your mama didn't raise no fool. Even if she married one."

"Oh Dad. These days they educate us about scams in school. Every scam has one thing in common: they sound too good to be true. They told us one of Madoff's secrets was to make his come-on sound exclusive. Like: just between you and me, you can get in on the ground floor of this deal of a lifetime—I'm offering the opportunity only to my closest friends and associates." He gulped. "From the names on this list it looks like Mr. Hammond was doing that too."

Early chuckled. "Finance, forensics, current events. Is there anything you're not into, Boy Wonder?"

"Thank you, thank you, Sam-I-Am," Tikki cried.

"Aren't you a little old for Dr. Seuss?"

"Oh, the places you'll go." Tikki giggled, but his crack was lost on his dad.

"What was in the hidden files?" Early asked.

"Letters. Most of them were to somebody named Taziz. Is that his wife?"

Uh oh, love letters. "Ah, she was one of Crystalline's suppliers."

"Huh? Siri's Seramics was the company's sole supplier," Tikki said.

"There was no mention of Taziz in the corporate records?"

"Nothing besides the letters."

Early pursed his lips. "She was also Hammond's girl-friend. Did you read the letters?"

"Enough to see what they were."

Worried, Early asked, "What did they say?"

"Porno type stuff. I love to caress your this and that, I want to kiss you all over, and such. Nothing I haven't seen online."

That all sounded irrelevant. Early decided to stick to the matter at hand. "Was there anything else company-related?"

"I found a few financial reports. There are some dividend figures on the spreadsheet but only for a few people." Tikki pulled up the file and ran his finger across the screen. "I found exact matches between the financial reports and the lines with dividend payouts on them."

Early checked out the open files on the screen. "You're right. It looks like Hammond sent reports only to the people who have dividends listed next to their names—four out of several dozen."

"Why would only four people get dividends? Nobody ever actually got them because of the 'reinvestment' angle, but you'd think he would at least list them on here. There are no others."

"Wait, what's this?" Early scanned the line for Hammond's sister and Tikki watched his father turn into a desk-pounding maniac. "Can Honoria be the *only* exception? There's no dividend notation for her on the spreadsheet and no corresponding financial report, yet we know her brother was paying her dividends in cash instead of 'reinvesting' them! Is she in on this scam too?"

Tikki gulped. "There's another letter in the hidden files

you should know about—it's to someone named Larry." He opened another document and read.

Dear Larry,

Sorry I had to send these with Taziz, but at the last minute I found out I couldn't make it. Enclosed you will find thirteen checks and money orders totaling $116,357.20. Please make sure they are all there and the total is correct! I suspect Taziz of being a little sticky-fingered at times. I know this shipment is light, but my cut will be the usual $25,000.

Cheers,
    Chandler

"He sent Taziz down to see Larry Bloch with checks and money orders and took a cut. What the hell were they up to?" He looked at Tikki. "The Madoff flag?"

Tikki nodded. "Maybe worse. And ya know what else?"

Early sat back and stared at the ceiling. "I'm not sure I can take anything else."

"There's no record of any bank accounts. Even ordinary people have a hard time getting along without a checking account."

"Siri told me he didn't trust banks. I'm guessing these files are his only financial records."

"Dad, I hate to say this but . . . there are way too many signs that Crystalline is bogus."

Wheels turned in Early's head. He heard Amber's voice

again: *Maybe Hammond and the dark-haired woman were in on something shady together.*

"I've got it!" Early leaped to his feet. "When Siri discovered Crystalline was a fraud and Taziz was in on the scam she flew into a rage and killed Hammond."

Tikki looked at his father as if Early had just crashed his Caprice through the living room wall. "Mr. Hammond was murdered?"

"Wait a minute," Early said, calming down. "Siri doesn't fly into rages." He thought of her ice-palace kitchen. Cold calculation was her style. And even if she did discover that Crystalline was a fraud, why murder her husband? She enjoyed being the wife of a wealthy guy and she didn't care how Hammond made his money. Maybe she was in on the fraud too. More likely she'd want to kill him *after* he ran off with the money.

Tikki's eyes were as big and bright as flying saucers. "What the hell are you talking about?"

Early placed a hand on his freaked-out son's shoulder. "Watch your mouth, young man. Suspicious company financials are not evidence of homicide. Actually, they're better proof that Hammond really did take off with his girlfriend. If those two were pulling a fast one and thought they were on the verge of being discovered their abrupt disappearance makes sense."

"You could be right. Except for this Bloch guy, it looks like Crystalline has had no new investors for months. A Ponzi scheme depends on new money coming in."

"Hammond wouldn't be the first to avoid arrest by vanishing. But now I don't know what to think. Murder or no murder?"

"I'd prefer no murder."

"Me too." Early stared at the flickering screen. Honoria's

name glowed back at him. He needed to talk to her again. "We'll sort this out."

"I hope by suppertime."

Early checked his watch. "Whoa, I told Taziz's landlady I'd be there at four to search her apartment. You've got your supper, I've gotta hustle." He grabbed his shabby trench coat and dashed out the door.

10

IN WHICH EARLY TAKES A TRIP TO NOWHERE WITH NOBODY

Early wedged his land yacht into a barely adequate parking spot in front of a well-kept duplex. A little old lady standing in the front yard stared at him. He figured she was either Taziz's landlady or someone locked out of her apartment.

He flashed a big toothy grin. She didn't run away screaming. "Are you Mr. Early?"

"Yes, ma'am." His huge body unfolded from the car. "You're Mrs. Leary?"

"Yes, deah. I have the key right here." She patted the pocket of her floral apron. Then, she held out her hand and smiled sweetly. "May I see your credentials?"

He handed over his ID, pleased that she wasn't as naïve as she had seemed.

She held his folder at arm's length, scrutinized it like she was reading her favorite novel, returned it, and said, "They seem to be in order. Follow me."

Early caught a glimpse of a smart little Smith and Wesson in her apron pocket. *No wonder she isn't scared. I better keep well behind her.*

She unlocked the door and Early paused to look around the front hall. The place seemed as sterile as a furniture showroom. Maybe Taziz only hung her virtual hat here? "Have you cleaned the apartment, Mrs. Leary?"

"No, I haven't touched a thing, deah. Isn't it nice and neat? Taziz was quite fastidious. But I suppose anyone's apartment would be tidy if they're never home."

"She wasn't here much?"

"I hardly ever saw her."

Early wondered where Taziz spent her time. This should have been the obvious meeting place for her and Hammond. They couldn't get it on at the mansion—Siri might have noticed something like that. Hammond's wife had seemed unconcerned about his affair, but she didn't give them her blessing either.

"This is how she left the place?"

"Yes. The deah girl bought out the lease too."

"How much time was left?"

"Six months."

"That's a lot to buy out. Do you have a copy of her check? It might provide some helpful information."

"I'm afraid not. She paid cash."

"Cash?" This neighborhood of former sea captains' mansions had been converted to condos or apartments when the houses became unaffordable for single families. Rents here weren't cheap.

"That's right, deah. Greenbacks. Moolah. Or what do the kids say these days? Benjamins?"

In other words, untraceable money. No wonder Mrs. Leary thought Taziz was a dear girl. "Have you rented the place out again?"

"Not yet. I don't know why she left her things behind, but if I have no word from her for a few months I'll box them up and put them into storage. I don't want to throw anything out. She was such a good tenant I'm hoping she'll come back."

A tenant who pays in cash and is never around—what's not to like? "Did she say where she was going?"

"No. I was in bed asleep when she moved out. The next day, I found a message on my phone saying her last payment was on the kitchen table with the key."

Slipping away in the night. Another good sign that Taziz and Hammond had run off with his money. *Then who was that woman I saw during the burglary? Obviously, she thought the money was still in the floor safe.*

Early was glad Mrs. Leary hadn't been a victim of whatever those two were trying to pull. "I'll get to work. You don't have to babysit me. This search could take quite a while."

"No problem. I'll be outside with a cup of tea. That deah girl brought the best tea with her from Iraq. Would you like some, Mr. Early?" She pulled a dainty porcelain cup from one of the sparkling white enamel cabinets.

"No, thanks. Did the dear girl always pay her rent on time?"

"She was very punctual." Mrs. Leary filled the teakettle and placed it on the stove.

"Was Chandler Hammond here often?"

She tilted her head. "Now that's a funny thing. I'm retired and I live right across the street and I often see who comes and goes. Everyone said Taziz was his girlfriend, but I recall seeing him here only once or twice. Not that I snoop you know." She pulled a teabag from a burlap sack and tossed it into her cup.

"Of course, you don't. Did anybody else visit her?"

"I don't think so since she usually wasn't here. Now, where did she keep the sugar?"

The situation kept getting stranger. If Taziz and Hammond weren't spending time here were they going to a motel? But why frequent a sleazy hot-sheet joint when she had such a nice apartment?

Maybe the guy gets off on sleaze. Maybe they had sex only on business trips. Or in the car? Eeww, have some class, Hammond. Get a room.

Early went upstairs. The master and spare bedrooms, both visible from the tiny hallway, looked unused. The spare bedroom held generic motel décor: plain lamps, standard furniture, and the usual bland pictures of mountains, woods, or beaches. No priceless artifacts here.

In the master bedroom, a few small posters of Middle East scenes were arranged in a circle around a larger one of a Baghdad sunset. The beautiful exotic views contrasted with the blah room. Early lingered to admire the dazzling golden spires and sun-washed palm trees. He was tempted to daydream about that nice warm place, but he had work to do.

He found nothing under the bed or furniture—not even dust. Then he tackled his most hated job: searching bureau drawers. Although he'd poked through other peoples' underwear for years, he still had to remind himself it was all part of the job.

But the heap of lingerie in Taziz's drawer was different—he'd never seen such an assortment of black lace. *I wonder if she has black lace shoes too.*

Since underwear drawers are favorite hiding places, he began pulling out the contents. His search was halted by a bright yellow silk teddy, much like one his wife had. Because his wife took all her clothing when she left, he savored the chance to feel the familiar silky material again.

He smiled and rubbed the teddy against his cheek, lost in memories.

The smell jarred him back to reality. Apparently, Taziz liked stinky expensive perfume.

Grossed out, he flung the teddy back into the drawer. He needed to focus on the case, not relive old times. Besides, this teddy belonged to a stranger. Even though he felt like he almost knew Taziz from groping her teddy in her bedroom, the chance of meeting her was remote.

The remaining drawers held only clothing and smelly sachets. Apparently, Taziz hadn't received the memo about favorite hiding places.

The walk-in closet held several dozen spike-heeled shoes placed neatly beneath matching designer dresses, but none of the shoes were black lace. *I'd sure like to see Hammond's credit card bill for this stuff.* Then he remembered Hammond didn't have any credit cards. The guy must have carried loads of cash to buy this caliber of clothing. If some lowlife knew that, Hammond could have been the victim of a robbery gone wrong. It was another possibility in a case that was more speculation than fact.

Early checked every shoe but found nothing, and the closet shelves were as barren as a department store after Christmas. He even searched the meager pockets of the designer dresses, useless for stashing anything bigger than a lipstick.

He scrutinized the master bath for signs of Hammond's presence; but there was no razor, no cologne, no men's clothing, not even a comb. He started to wonder if Mrs. Leary had brought him to the right apartment. The clothes in the closet and bureau seemed to be the only indication anybody had lived here. How could a home be this barren?

And if Taziz left all her clothes behind—including her underwear—did they run away to a nude beach?

He wasn't ready to give up. Taziz must have forgotten something. Then, more pay dirt turned up—he pulled open the nightstand drawer and found another flash drive.

Early smiled and slipped the drive into his pocket. There was no writing on the outside. He hoped it wasn't just a copy of Hammond's drive . . . or worse, blank.

Mrs. Leary shuffled into the room in her fuzzy pink slippers. "Did you find anything, deah?"

"Just lots of clothes," he lied.

She glanced around. "You made quite a mess, Mr. Early."

The place looked undisturbed to him. But to stay on her good side he said, "Sorry ma'am. As I like to say, always do what you're best at."

She let out a hearty laugh. "Never mind deah, I'll tidy up later."

"You haven't heard from Taziz? Not even about what to do with her stuff?"

"Not a word. And she didn't leave any instructions in her message. Seems very strange for someone who took such good care of her belongings."

He handed her his card. "Please let me know if you do hear from her or you think of anything else important."

"I certainly will, deah." She lowered her voice. "Mr. Early? Do you think anything bad happened to Taziz? And that nice Mr. Hammond?"

"At this point, I've seen no evidence of that." He paused. "You thought Hammond was nice? Didn't you say you never met him?"

She blushed. "Yes, I did say that. I didn't want to seem nosy."

"I don't think you're nosy, Mrs. Leary." Early thanked his

good fortune for nosy people. "You're just watching out for your property."

"That's right, deah." She beamed at his positive spin on her nosiness.

She's gonna cave. Damn, I'm good.

"Mr. Hammond seemed congenial. He waved at me the last time I saw him."

"When was that?"

"A few weeks ago. Right before Taziz left."

"But you didn't speak to him."

"No," she said. "He was parked in front of the house, waiting for Taziz. When I called hello from my yard, he gave me a friendly wave."

"And this was during the day."

"Yes."

"Could you tell what kind of mood he was in?"

"I didn't see his face but the wave seemed cheerful."

Probably just got laid. Why wouldn't he be cheerful? "Thanks. I'll search the downstairs now."

"All right. I'll be on the porch with my tea."

He turned his attention to the kitchen, which looked generic—he had seen high school cafeterias with more personality. The kitchen equipment and food in the fully stocked cabinets seemed untouched. Even the kettle Mrs. Leary had boiled water in seemed like it had just come off the store shelf.

How could anybody live like this? Forensics revealed that even the cleanest person leaves signs of their presence on their environment. Did Taziz never eat here? Did she always get takeout? But the flatware looked pristine too. Maybe she used plastic utensils and paper plates and tossed them instead of cleaning up. Was she lazy . . . or destroying DNA?

He checked the kitchen trash can and found a brand-new liner. *Just my luck that the trash can is the only thing Mrs. Leary cleaned.*

The beige tile fireplace also looked unused—no soot fell out when he opened the damper. He dropped and crawled into the firebox, twisting to look up the chimney. An unused chimney was another favorite if risky hiding place, but he saw only clear sky.

This was a tough search. Nothing was in the usual hiding places; he figured Taziz took the important stuff with her, which meant she didn't plan to return.

Another hour passed and he came up empty. The apartment had barely told him anything about Taziz let alone Hammond. He pinned his hopes on the flash drive from her bedroom.

He began to wonder about Taziz. He knew what she smelled like and what she wore but what did she look like? Did she have brothers or sisters? Was she really just after Hammond's money? The internet search he did on her had revealed nothing. It was almost as if she didn't exist.

Such a mysterious and intriguing woman. She shows up here in Maine, plugs herself into a life, and then unplugs just as easily and vanishes.

Early figured Mrs. Leary might have some more answers. He found her asleep on a wooden glider bench on the porch and gently shook her by the shoulder. "Psst, Mrs. Leary?"

She awoke with a start, spilling the teacup on the side table, her hand going for the gun in her apron.

Another woman with a gun. Once again, Early jumped back, but this time he reached skyward. Mrs. Leary shook her head, and then smiled as she looked up and recognized him. "Oh, I'm sorry. It's nice and warm out here, I must have dozed off. I feel a bit foolish."

Early put his hands down and exhaled. "It is a beautiful day and this porch looks like a great place for a nap."

She stared off into the distance. "Sometimes I'd see Taziz napping out here."

"Hard to believe she was home long enough to take a nap."

"Once in a while, she'd sit out here waiting for Mr. Hammond to pick her up."

"In his fancy Bentley, eh? His car goes well with the neighborhood." Early chuckled.

Mrs. Leary's brow wrinkled. "Is a Bentley one of those big SUV things? That's what he drove."

Now Early's brow wrinkled. "You saw him in an SUV, not a car?"

She nodded. "A big black one."

Early wondered why Hammond would pick up his girlfriend in his wife's SUV. Maybe he really did like to have sex in the car. But the Bentley had plenty of room and was probably more comfortable.

Great Hitchens' ghost, how much of a bastard is this guy? Cheating his sister, having sex with his girlfriend in his wife's SUV—the case was starting to sound like a sick joke.

The thought of Hammond and Taziz getting frisky in Siri's SUV shook Early back to business. "Can you tell me any more about Taziz? What she looked like, any odd habits she had?"

The landlady pursed her lips. "I don't recall any quirks, but I was never around her much. As for what she looked like: long legs, long black hair, beautiful brown eyes . . ."

That was too generic for Early. "Can you be more specific? Any tattoos or distinguishing features?"

Mrs. Leary sighed. "I suppose I would have noticed more about her if I were a man."

Early snickered. Taziz sounded like quite the femme fatale. "Thanks. I'm going to call it a day."

"Feel free to visit any time. And let me know if you have a friend who's looking for a nice place to rent."

Early smiled. That was hospitable of her. Opportunistic too. "I sure will. Bye."

Early waved as he walked to his car. He sat in the front seat wondering why on earth Honoria wanted her brother back. Perhaps she didn't know what he was really like. Or maybe she wanted to ream him because her dividend was late. Neither possibility was inconceivable.

11

IN WHICH HONORIA GETS INTO A SNIT. AGAIN.

E arly hoped Honoria wasn't home but that would just postpone the inevitable. If he didn't talk to her now, she'd call him—again—to ask his progress. Which was none.

He hesitated, and then rang the doorbell.

Honoria opened the door. "It's about time you made an appearance. I was just about to call you. What have you found out?"

He cringed. "Can we talk inside?"

"Sure."

"No barking dog today?" He looked into the hall.

"He's on vacation."

She seemed in a good mood. Early followed her into the living room, sat down, and began recording with his cell phone.

"That thing again? Where's the cosmetician you said you would bring?" Honoria poured coffee from a gold-edged porcelain pot.

"I tried to find one, but they were all on vacation."

She picked up her cup, smiled, and settled back on the sofa. "What have you got to report?"

"We've found some documentation on Crystalline, but we need a few days to give it a thorough examination."

"That's encouraging." She took a sip of coffee, put down her cup, and leaned in. "Let's hear the rest."

"Our investigation is moving along." The words sounded lame to him even as they left his lips. "The police found your brother's cell phone was still in use after his disappearance."

"Good news indeed," she gushed. Then, her face clouded. "Wait. If he's been using the phone, why hasn't he returned my calls? Or even picked up his messages—I've checked every day, but his voice mailbox is still at full capacity."

Early stared at the floor and bit his lip. "Honoria . . . after he disappeared, there were some calls between him and Siri—"

"*What?* He was talking to that little bitch? And she was talking to *him* after she told me and everybody else that she doesn't know where he is?"

She jumped up and stomped around the room. "Dammit, I knew she was lying, but Chandler? He calls her and just leaves me hanging? That bastard!" She shook a finger at Early. "I'll bet Siri really does know where he is. I ought to—"

"Honoria, settle down." Early arose and tried to calm her, but his efforts were like déjà vu all over again.

"Son of a bitch. Don't you tell me to settle down," she snarled, waving her arms. "What kind of bullshit is this? When did I become a nobody? Chandler and Siri are having nice little chats while I twist in the wind wondering where the hell he is and hoping he's not chained to a steam pipe.

How could he do this to me after what our family has been through? He should know better. Did he forget what it was like? The waiting, the agony?" Her hands formed fists. "Ooohhh, now I want to kick both of them right in their inconsiderate asses."

"That's how I feel, too, Honoria. Siri told me the same lies."

Honoria stopped pacing and frowned. "And this surprised you? I informed you she was a liar at our very first interview. Now do you believe me?" She glared up at him, hands on her hips.

He tried a shy smile. "I like to make up my own mind."

That didn't impress Honoria. "Fine, but you need to give more consideration to people who know the real facts. Like me."

"I admit you were right about Siri." He folded his arms. "But Honoria, have you ever thought your brother might not want anybody to know where he is?"

She strode over to him, pulled herself up as far as she could, and growled into his broad chest, "What's that supposed to mean? I'm not anybody; I'm his sister. Why the hell would he hide from me?"

How could he tell this crazy woman that her brother was a crook? She might go even more ballistic if that was possible. The evidence of Hammond's guilt seemed solid to him but dodging a swarm of blackflies would be easier. "Any speculations I make about that would be premature."

"Premature, eh? They had better mature damn quick." Her tone was colder than a blizzard on Mount Katahdin.

"Please, sit down, Honoria. We'll discuss that matter, I promise." Early counted on his melodious baritone to smooth her ruffled feathers. "Right now, I have some important questions."

"Questions, questions, questions. I want answers, not more questions." She pointed her finger at him and hissed, "I hope you know what you're doing, Mr. Early."

"What I'm doing," he grumbled, "is my best."

She simmered down just a bit. "Yes. Yes, of course it is. But if you're wrong . . . well, I don't have to tell you that the consequences will be dire." She flopped onto the sofa, picked up her coffee cup, sat back, and stared at him. "Go ahead."

"You said you invested in your brother's company, the Crystalline Art Distributorship."

"At least you've got something right."

Early gritted his teeth. Ignoring her digs wouldn't be easy even though he understood how she felt. "Tell me again how much you invested?"

"Fifty thousand dollars."

That was the same figure he had seen beside her name in the file on the flash drive. She had just driven the final nail into Crystalline's sleazy coffin.

Great Hitchens' ghost, he really did scam his own sister. Now I do want to find him, just so Hal can throw his worthless ass in jail.

The case had turned into a rat's nest. Honoria hadn't been concerned about her brother's disappearance until her dividend went missing with him. Hammond was scamming everybody he could. His wife might have killed him. And what happened to his girlfriend? The company initials CAD were a fitting irony. Chandler Hammond wasn't the richest of the filthy rich, but he was one of the filthiest.

Early started digging for more documentation on the black hole called Crystalline. "Did you ever receive a prospectus or any other kind of information on Crystalline?"

She let out a rich-girl snort. "Why would I need a prospectus for a company run by my own brother?"

Oh brother. I wouldn't trust my *brother with fifty grand. But that's probably chump change to Honoria.* "Ever get any annual reports?"

"No."

"Never?"

She rolled her eyes. "No, Early, never."

"Did you ever request information on the company?"

"Of course not. I didn't need any."

"And you had no input into company operations?"

She stared at the ceiling and sighed as if she were talking to an obtuse customer service rep, then lowered her eyes and seethed, "Mr. Early. My brother is a financier. He knows more about these things than I do. I don't interfere with his business. As long as Chandler came by every month with my regular dividend, I had no issues with the way he ran his company. As far as I'm concerned Crystalline was doing just fine until he disappeared."

Early shook his head. *And I'm sure Hammond counted on all his investors to think exactly the same thing.*

12

IN WHICH EARLY FOREGOES CHEAP THRILLS . . . ALMOST

Early settled into the worn vinyl chair in his tiny office. Honoria's foul play theory still didn't seem plausible. He thought it more likely that some of Crystalline's investors had become suspicious and started asking questions. That would have brought the whole Ponzi scheme crashing down on Hammond's head—enough incentive to make anybody disappear.

A wild idea popped into Early's mind: did Hammond stage his own murder? It had happened in similar scandals. But then why didn't he leave more convincing evidence?

What supported Siri's story that Hammond had run off with Taziz? The missing money—but was any money left to be missing? Then there was the Bentley at the airport unless Siri had planted it as a red herring.

He dialed the cop shop. Jeremy answered the phone. "Didja smoke out the real story yet?"

Early could almost see the smirk on Jeremy's freckled face. "I'm dealing with a huge smokescreen and I need more answers. Was Hammond driving when you saw his car pull out of his driveway on the night he disappeared?"

"Beats me. His SUV has those blacked-out windows."

"Wait, you saw Siri's SUV, not the Bentley?"

"Definitely the SUV. Not the Bentley."

"Why would he be driving his wife's car?"

"I guess he likes those blacked-out windows for extracurricular activities with his girlfriend." Jeremy chuckled. "Maybe Siri was driving. All I saw was the SUV."

"But the driver was in a big hurry?"

"Damn skippy. Tore out like they had a bear behind."

"Always a possibility in these parts. Did you see any other cars leave the house?"

"No, but I had no reason to stake the place out. Nothing seemed suspicious and I had just put in a long night due to that feed store robbery."

"Lotta brush fires that night, huh?"

"Where there's smoke."

Early hung up. That pesky SUV was showing up everywhere. Did Hammond and Taziz leave in the Bentley and what Jeremy saw was Siri going after them? But in her interview, Siri said she never saw her husband again after going to bed. Did she catch them and kill them, and then go to bed when she returned home? Nah—she'd have to hide the bodies, clean up the blood, maybe even get the Bentley to the airport. Siri wasn't enough of a mastermind to pull off something this complicated. If a simple question from him had caused her to spill her coffee he couldn't imagine her handling the kind of bloody mess a murder can make without involving her staff.

On the other hand, Early had already discovered aspects of Siri he couldn't have imagined.

He locked his office and left for home to see what else Tikki had come up with, endless questions following him all the way.

Early came in the front door, tossed his coat onto the couch, and yelled, "Honey, I'm home." He knew Tikki hated that, which made it perfect payback for those damn video games.

A moan came from the spare room. Early chuckled. Mission accomplished. "Anything else on the flash drive?"

"Nothing useful."

"That's okay." Early sat down to check the file, but the cursor went wild, dashing all over the screen. The cat was playing with the mouse again.

"We really need a tablet. Shoo, CC." Tikki waved at the cat, but she wouldn't give up her prize.

"Why don't you ask Santa for one?"

"I just did."

"As if. What's CC?"

"Computer cat." Tikki chuckled as he pried the mouse from her claws.

"Uh . . . okay. I need you to copy the flash drive so I can return the original before Siri gets back. Oh, I found another one in Taziz's apartment." He walked to the couch and pulled the drive from his trench coat pocket.

Tikki sighed and stretched across the desk. "Dad, puh-leeze, I've been staring at this computer for hours. I'm getting cross-eyed, I need a break."

"Me too." Early handed him the new drive.

Tikki switched drives in the USB port and pulled up a list of files. "Why don't you take over? I'm really hungry." He pointed at the screen. "Here's the list of files on the drive. Double-clicking on one launches the program that opens it."

Early stared dubiously at the screen. He was no techno-geek, and sometimes computers were a mystery to this detective. "I'm used to the laptop your mother took with her. Does this one work the same way?"

"It should. If the file doesn't open, a dialog box will pop up to say the system doesn't recognize that kind of document. Just close the box and try another file."

Early's look went from dubious to confused. "Aren't all the files the same? If the system doesn't recognize one why would it recognize another?"

"Dad, you're so suspicious," Tikki wailed, rolling his head. "Don't panic, I'll be back in a few minutes." He dashed off, leaving his father to sink or swim in the digital waters.

Early scanned the list of files. They were all pictures with numbers assigned by the camera instead of titles. He shooed away the persistent cat, grabbed the mouse, and double-clicked on the first file.

A photo filled the screen. "Yay me," he crowed as he saw Siri smiling and sitting pretty on a concrete bench in her pristine backyard . . . with the beautiful woman who had almost shot him at the Hammond mansion.

He blinked. She was the same woman all right—same exotic long black hair and nice rack. But who was she and how did she know Siri?

He clicked on the next file and saw Siri still sitting next to the mystery woman. But now they were locking lips.

Great Hitchens' ghost, what the hell?

The next picture was even more revealing—literally. The mystery woman had pulled Siri's frilly white blouse off her shoulders.

Early began clicking furiously. Now the woman's face was buried in Siri's lustrous neck; now she was undoing Siri's black lace bra; now her hand was cupping one of Siri's bare breasts, the nipple staring out at him like a one-eyed barn owl.

A dozen more pictures were on the drive. Early had caught fire even though he started to feel somewhat slimy. Was Siri trying to break into porn? Was Taziz the mystery woman or the photographer? Taziz was involved somehow —why else would this flash drive be in her apartment? He wished he knew what Taziz looked like.

He skipped to the last picture, and then whispered, "Great Hitchens' ghost." In his semi-wild youth, he and his friends had idly wondered how two women could manage to do something like what he saw them doing. Now the mystery was solved and the answer looked rather acrobatic.

He heard footsteps. Early fumbled for the mouse and quickly closed the picture. He didn't know who the woman was, but he knew *what* she was: Siri's girlfriend. Or Siri's afternoon delight. He wondered if Hammond knew his wife was engaging in the same activities as he was. Hell, maybe Hammond had taken the pictures.

The real question was whether the photos had any connection to Hammond's disappearance. Did Siri get rid of her husband to be with her girlfriend? Divorce might have left her broke and Siri would never stand for that. Honoria's suspicions were looking better.

Tikki walked into the room with a sandwich and a cup of coffee. "Howzit goin', Dad? Open any of those files?" He sat down and tucked into his food.

"Yeah."

"What did you find?"

"There were some pictures."

"Pictures of what?" Tikki stopped in mid-munch to pick up the mouse.

"No!" Early grabbed the mouse.

Tikki jumped. "What's up with you?"

Early released the mouse and shifted in discomfort. How to proceed now? "Uh, Tikki, we need to have a talk."

His son stared at him aghast. "You mean the sex talk?" He tried not to choke on his food. "Right now?"

Early wished his wife were still around. He was sure she'd be much better at this.

Tikki sighed and put down his sandwich. "Okay. What do you wanna know about sex?"

Once again Early was glad he hadn't sipped his coffee yet—it wasn't easy to clean spewed coffee off a keyboard. "I don't want to know anything," he growled. "I'm supposed to teach *you* about it."

"Right." The boy snickered, and then grew suspicious. "Does your sudden interest in sex have anything to do with the pictures on that drive?"

"Um, they were family photos."

"Family photos? What kind of family is that? Should we call the cops?"

"No. You're right, the pictures are pretty sleazy, but the people in them are consenting adults. Like I've told you, it's different when you're thirteen."

Tikki grinned. "Then I can't wait to consent."

Early suspected Tikki had seen worse on the internet. But exposing his son to those pictures wasn't appropriate, especially when the people in them were parties in a case. "We don't need a copy of this flash drive, son. Taziz left it behind, so I'll give it to Chief Hal."

He pulled the flash drive from the port. Hal could get his jollies checking out those pictures later. They might be evidence, but of what? That Siri and her hot date killed Hammond in order to get married? He'd heard of similar situations, but Early had trouble seeing Siri as a murderer. He still thought murder was too messy for her.

He wanted to take a shower. He felt like he'd been peeking through a bedroom keyhole. Surveillance was part of his job, but he never went inside a motel or house or looked into the windows. There was no need: courts could deduce the activity inside from the photos or videos he took outside. He wanted to see only what was necessary to close the case.

At least now he knew why Taziz's apartment was empty. She probably spent all her time at the mansion—with Siri, not Hammond. Everyone assumed Taziz went along on his trips, but if she was the woman in the pictures maybe she was spending time with Siri while he was gone. Did Hammond only *think* Taziz was his girlfriend but she was really Siri's? If so, no way did she run away with him. The woman in the pictures looked like she'd rather run away with Siri.

If Taziz hadn't gone off with Hammond was she still around? And if so, where would she be?

Maybe the Hammond family camp held some answers. He needed to get up there.

13

IN WHICH THE CASE BEGINS TO HAVE TEETH

Early decided to pay Siri a surprise visit upon her return from California. Smoke again filled the mansion's backyard as he cruised up the long winding driveway, but this time he sauntered behind the house. Siri was pulling a pot from a trash can and wearing the same white blouse he had seen in the photos.

He stopped short. *Great Hitchens' ghost, I need to forget about those pictures and focus.*

Siri turned to face him, her blouse shimmering in the slight breeze. "Oh, Mr. Early, I'm glad you're here."

"You are?" He struggled not to think about what was underneath that blouse.

"I'm all alone and I can't empty these trash cans by myself. You'll help me, won't you?" She flashed what she must have considered a winning smile. He wondered if a murderer could put on such a cheesy act.

The things I do for this job. "I'll help, but I have some more questions for you."

"We can deal with those later. Right now, the trash cans are more important. Come with me." She marched him to the swimming pool and dunked the hot pot she held in her tongs, sending steam hissing everywhere. Having no desire for a facial, Early choked and waved his hands.

Siri pulled out the pot, set it aside, and pointed to a large gray mound near the swimming pool. "That pile is where we dump the ashes after the raku process is finished." She pushed a trash can toward him and indicated several others beside the shed. "All these cans need to be emptied. Please make sure they are completely cleaned out. Any residue causes unforeseen results in the glaze, which can ruin the entire batch of pottery."

Yes'm, I'ma tote dat can. She sure is used to giving orders.

With a mighty grunt, he hauled the heavy can to the pile, looking for a dumping spot that wouldn't require further lifting. He flipped the can over and pounded on the bottom to ensure it was completely cleaned out, thank you very much, Ma'am.

A glimmering white object cascaded out of the ashes and rolled onto the grass. *What is that? Looks like . . . nah.*

He picked it up and peered at it. *I was right, it's a tooth.*

Early had gained a bit of knowledge about raku from Siri, but he didn't recall her mentioning teeth as a glaze additive. Whose tooth was this and how did it come to be in the ashes? And most importantly, had its donor been willing?

He slipped the tooth into his pocket. He didn't want to let Siri know he had found it. Discretion was always the wisest choice.

As he dragged the empty can back to the shed, he noticed a large red cooler beside a pile of empty tinfoil boxes, its lid open to the warm afternoon sun. It looked about the same size as the one he had found in Hammond's safe. Due to the Glock-toting beauty who had interrupted his investigation, he couldn't be sure it was the same one.

He checked inside the cooler, hoping to find a stray plastic bag, but it was empty. Running his hands around the interior yielded nothing although his nose detected an odd smell—vaguely familiar yet not quite identifiable.

Humming a cheery tune, Siri trotted around the corner of the shed; then, she turned pale when she saw Early with his hands in the cooler. He thought she was about to faint and stood up to catch her, but she stayed on her feet and gasped, fanning her wide-eyed face. "Sorry, I got a little woozy for a moment. I must have inhaled too much smoke." She took a few deep breaths. "I keep some of my glaze additives in that cooler."

Early found her statement odd. Why explain the cooler when he hadn't asked about it? A person with guilty knowledge would do that. But guilty knowledge of what?

Before she could demand that he haul more ashes, he quickly asked, "Can we go up to the house? I really need to talk to you."

She rolled her eyes. "If you insist, I guess the ashes can wait."

Once again, he followed her up the Belgian block path to the mansion. "What are those blue flowers growing near the house?" he asked. "I really like them."

Siri looked surprised but pleased that he was admiring something of hers. "I don't know. The gardener planted them."

"I'd like to have some for my son. He loves to garden, especially flowers." Early worked hard to make a fuss even Siri would notice. "Could I dig up one or two? I promise not to make a mess."

"I'd rather dig them up for you. Be right back." She headed for the garage.

"I'll wait in the office," he shouted.

His ploy had worked. In seconds he was through the French doors of Hammond's office. He dashed to the huge safe, spun the dial, pulled open the door, and tossed Siri's flash drive onto the shelf. But before he could see if the cooler was still inside, he heard Siri's footsteps coming up the walkway.

She's a fast one in many ways. He closed the safe's door, spun the dial, and strolled back to the French doors to watch Siri break a sweat digging up a few blue flowers. He thanked her profusely and put them in his car. She had no idea what he really was thankful for.

They walked down the hall to the ice palace kitchen. The glass table appeared untouched since his last visit. He threw his trench coat over an empty chair again. Making coffee at the counter, Siri scowled a little less than she had last time.

He sat down and began recording with his cell phone. Siri brought the coffee cups over and settled into a chair. This scenario was becoming quite familiar. Would things be more productive this time?

"I have more questions about Crystalline," he said.

Siri wrinkled her nose, twirling a strand of her long blonde hair around her finger.

"You said Crystalline sells your pottery?" Early asked.

"I produce the art, Chandler sells it. That's how things work, which is just fine with me." She took a sip of coffee.

"How are your pottery sales doing?"

"Very good, according to Chandler. All I know is my pottery runs always sell out even at the big shows. Chandler has placed my work into finer shops, homes, and galleries worldwide."

Early was amused by how she loved to brag. He tried fishing—Maine style with a trap. "You seem familiar with Crystalline's marketing, but you know nothing about the investment end of the business?"

"Finances are entirely Chandler's baby." She smiled and waved her hands. "He's always looking for new investors. Money men will be money men, after all. But I'm afraid financial details are just too complicated for an artist like me."

She was practically tying herself into a yoga knot trying to convince him of her complete ignorance. She didn't seem to realize how suspicious her toe-in-the-sand act sounded.

Early swirled his coffee. His trap had made Siri uncomfortable but that was about all. How could he crumble this tough cookie? Siri was writing the script and she was smart enough to realize nobody could get past "I don't know."

But surely, he was smarter? When did he start giving up this easily? *Use your brain, man. Go after what you want.* "I asked to interview your staff. Are they around?"

"No." She drew circles on the spotless glass tabletop with one blood-red fingernail. "Everybody's gone."

His jaw dropped. "You fired them while they were on vacation?"

She stared at the ceiling. "Couldn't be helped. I was out of money."

Of course. Siri hadn't had a chance to tell them what to say and when to shut up. That's all in the script. She had taken command of the script and was stonewalling. He gritted his teeth but kept his cool and looked around the immaculate kitchen. "Who's taking care of the place?"

"The boy down the street mows the lawn and I'm

cleaning around the house a little. I haven't had a chance to consider my options yet. The whole situation is just . . . overwhelming." She gagged as if she were about to cry.

Early must have looked astonished because Siri straightened up and took another sip of coffee. She tried a save, sighing. "Just have to take one day at a time I guess."

"Do you have phone numbers for your former staff members?"

He could see her writing the script again. "Well, the gardener said he was going back to Mexico. His wife was our maid and I suppose she went with him. The caretaker had already left for his family's home in St. Lucia."

Although he could guess the answer, he asked, "And you have no contact information for any of them?"

She shrugged. "I have no reason to contact them. For all I know, there are no phones wherever they are now."

And thus, her script tied up the loose ends into a nice neat bow for his convenience. Early wanted to jump across the table and throttle her. Because she was a woman, he buried his brief violent urge. His mama would have been proud.

Now what? He had to think outside the script, so he tried changing the channel. "Was your husband acting differently before his disappearance?"

She pursed her lips. "Different how?"

"Nervous, jumpy, anxious? Or the opposite —depressed?"

"He wasn't nervous and he never seems depressed."

Early couldn't disguise his sarcasm. "Was there any unusual behavior that you *did* notice?"

Siri ignored his tone as she swirled her coffee. "He seemed a bit distracted. And he's been rather disorganized lately. He keeps losing things."

"What kind of things?"

"Business papers, things like that."

"Losing business papers sounds pretty serious." *Not to mention convenient considering what we know now.* "Papers concerning Crystalline?"

"I guess. Crystalline is his only business that I know of."

Early found her answer unusual. "Do you think he has some other business you *don't* know of?"

She sipped her coffee, smiled, and said, "For all I know, he does. Chandler doesn't discuss business with me. He realizes that stuff goes over my head."

Obviously, Siri was still trying to show how uninvolved she was with Crystalline but she wasn't fooling Early. Lots of guys liked to tell every detail about themselves to anybody whether people listened or not; Hammond had probably told her quite a lot about Crystalline. Judging from the smokescreen she was trying very hard to create—and not just from her pots—she knew the truth.

"Could he have mentioned something about his business that you've forgotten?"

She grimaced. "How can I tell you about something I've forgotten?"

She was right, but he felt like punching something. He sat back to cool off.

"My pottery is all I think about these days." Siri sighed. "It helps me deal with Chandler's disappearance."

That almost sounded like regret. Was she losing control of the script? He hoped so. "Have you had another chance to go through his office?"

"Yes. Everything important is gone except for the flash drive in the safe. And that's just personal stuff."

Early lowered his head to hide a smile.

"I guess Chandler didn't want to take it along when he

ran off with Taziz. She'd probably be annoyed to have reminders of his former life lying around."

Early was puzzled. Hammond's laptop and phone were gone, but everything concerning Crystalline was still here, even the money in the safe—how could he have forgotten that?

Being dead could explain it. As the saying goes, you can't take it with you.

"Does he keep anything off-premises in a safe-deposit box or storage unit?"

"I doubt it. There are no storage facilities near here and I couldn't find any bank papers."

That confirmed Tikki's finding of no existing bank accounts. "How could he run a business without a bank account?"

"Chandler says he doesn't want banks snooping into his personal effects. He values his privacy quite highly."

Yeah, scammers are like that. "What makes him think they would? Banks don't snoop into safe-deposit boxes unless they're served with a search warrant." Early leaned forward. "Could he have been involved in something that wasn't legit?"

Siri's eyes widened. She lowered them to study her perfect California manicure, and then shook her head. "I don't know why Chandler does the things he does. That's just his way. Maybe it's a tax dodge?" She looked up at him. "He conducts his business affairs in his own manner. Nothing he said made sense to me. Eventually, I stopped asking."

He had a good reason to conduct his business affairs that way. Early considered confronting Siri with the tooth he had found to see if that would shake up this ice cream float. But he had the feeling he should hold back.

Siri yawned. "Are we done here, Mr. Early?"

"One more question. Why did you say you hadn't heard from your husband since his disappearance?"

Her eyes became ice crystals, matching the kitchen decor. "Because I hadn't."

Early pulled a sheet of paper from his pocket. "We obtained his cell phone records. Calls were made from his phone to yours several times after his disappearance."

"That's true," she said with a sinister purr.

Early nearly fainted. He wasn't expecting a confirmation.

"Somebody did call my phone, but it wasn't Chandler."

"Who was it?"

"I don't know. Whenever I answered no one was on the line."

"Did you report this to the police?" he asked.

"Why? Is calling somebody a crime?"

"You didn't think that was suspicious?"

"Why would I? Maybe he lost his phone and some kid found it and thought it would be fun to troll the people in the directory."

"People usually discontinue service when they lose their phones." He checked the sheet. "The only calls from his phone after he vanished were to you."

"Why should I do the police's job for them? I don't even know why they'd investigate Chandler's disappearance except to shut up his sister."

Early wanted to say investigating was what the police did, and making information easier to collect would help them do their job better, but that would be lost on Siri. "Why do you think you got those calls?"

"I don't know; they never left a message. Whenever I called Chandler his voice mailbox was full and, eventually, I gave up."

Early looked at the cell phone records and raised his eyebrows. "Some of those calls were several minutes long. But you didn't talk to anyone and there were no messages?"

"That's right. No voice messages and no texts."

"I find that hard to believe."

"You can find it any way you want. All I know is I heard a great deal of nothing on my voicemail."

Early frowned. "Why would somebody leave blank messages?"

Siri stared into her coffee cup. "I suspected it was Taziz calling to taunt me."

"Why wouldn't she call you on her own phone?"

"Because she knew I wouldn't answer. But I'd answer if Chandler called."

"Did you save any of the messages?"

She looked at him as if his brain had fallen out of his head and landed in a huge bloody mess on her virginal glass tabletop. "Why would I save empty voicemail messages?"

As usual, Siri's merry-go-round logic was making Early dizzy. He wanted to get off the carousel, take the intriguing tooth, and hit the road.

"Does he use social media?"

Siri laughed. "Putting his secrets on the internet for the world to see? You must be kidding. That's the last thing he'd ever do."

Early rubbed the scar on his chin as he regarded her. "Did he ever mention the name Larry Bloch?"

He could swear she froze up just a teeny bit. But everything in the kitchen was already so frozen, it was just a matter of degree. In seconds she was back to her usual flighty act.

"No. I don't believe he ever has."

Early gave up. "Okay, I think that's all I need for now.

Thanks for your time, Mrs. Hammond." He shut off his phone.

"Goodbye, Mr. Early. Please let me know if you have any more questions."

As if you would give me any answers.

14

IN WHICH EARLY SEES THE ELEPHANT IN THE ROOM

A discouraged private investigator, Early walked into his office, heard a noise behind him, and turned to see Amber waving a feather duster around her reading room across the hall. He recalled the card showing the dark-haired woman who was hiding something. Siri was hiding something—maybe several somethings—but as Amber had pointed out, Siri was blonde. If the card referred to Siri, what explained the discrepancy? If it didn't, who did the card indicate? He wanted answers, and he knew only one way to get them.

"Hi, Amber. Spring cleaning?"

She sneezed. "Incense produces a great atmosphere for readings but leaves a lot of dust."

"Gesundheit. But isn't that what people expect when they go to see a psychic? Dusty, musty, and dim?"

Amber shook her head, her chandelier earrings swinging and sparkling. "Next you'll be telling me to dress up like an old gypsy. When are you going to make that giant leap into the twentieth century? Modern tarot readers aren't like the fortune-tellers you see in those old horror movies."

"I'll leap when I start liking its looks."

"I think it's too late for that. How's Honoria's case going?"

He pursed his lips. "Remember that card depicting the dark-haired woman who's hiding something? I still like Siri for that, but I can't get past the dark hair."

Amber put down her feather duster. "I'm expecting a client in fifteen minutes but that gives us enough time to do a one-card reading. Maybe we can clear this up." She sat down at her reading table and retrieved her tarot deck from the drawer.

Early sat across from her. "Shall I shuffle?"

She fanned the cards across the table, face up. "First, check out my new deck, *The Alchemical Tarot.* How do you like it? The images go back to tarot's original roots, a medieval mnemonic picture system for people who couldn't read, which included just about everybody those days." She chuckled.

Early eyed the cards. Their pictures ranged from ordinary—a man stamping out coins in his workshop—to bizarre, a dog on fire. He picked one up and said, "The King of Cups as a whale? Who'da thunk it?"

"In this deck, he's the King of Vessels. We usually do think of him as human, but the symbolism here is quite different from the traditional Rider-Waite deck most readers use."

"I'll say. There are lots of naked women."

"Modern tarot decks allow more freedom of expression and variety in the artwork."

"I can hardly wait to see the one card I get to pull. I hope it's a naked woman. With dark hair, of course." Early winked.

Amber gathered the cards and presented the deck to him. He gave the deck a good shuffle and handed it back.

She fanned the cards across the table, face down this time. "Keep your mind on your question, pull out one card, and turn it over."

Early chose a card and flipped it face up in eager anticipation, but the picture sent a chill through him. The card showed four clay pots. Balancing on them was an elephant, each of its feet atop one of their long slender necks. "What the hell is this?"

She studied the card, and then looked at Early, bemused. "The four of vessels. I was just explaining to you that cups are vessels in—"

His eyes were wild. "I can see that. Tell me what it means."

Amber's jaw dropped. She stared at him. "Why are you going ballistic? It's just a card."

He leaned back, threw up his hands, and took a deep breath. "Sorry, I didn't realize how I must have sounded. You know Siri is a pottery artist, right?"

"No, I didn't. Are these pots like the ones she makes? Is that why the card is disturbing you?"

"No, her pots are much fancier than the ones on this card. But the elephant standing on them looks . . . ominous. You're right, this deck is disturbing. Even the naked women are disturbing."

"The deck is a phantasmagoria. The cards depict the images that formed in the alchemist's mind."

"I wonder what he was smoking."

"Probably sulfur fumes. Or he might have had mercury poisoning. Either one can produce some pretty crazy images. Until they killed him, anyway."

"Alchemy sounds pretty dangerous. Tell me, what's your interpretation of this card?"

She ran her finger over the card. "The elephant is on a

beach. You can see the ocean behind him, and sand and beach grass at the bottom of the picture. Sand shifts and tides ebb and flow, reminding us that things are constantly changing. But the four of vessels . . . I interpret fours as 'you need to,' and vessels symbolize emotions. Someone may be feeling a great deal of emotional pressure, similar to what the vessels feel from the elephant. In short, it looks like this person needs to deal with the elephant in the room."

He raised his eyebrows. "And you think that person is me?"

"You nearly had a meltdown when you saw the card. I can tell a lot about clients from their reactions."

"What can you tell from mine?"

"You're way stressed out. I told you Honoria would get to you. That woman is like a jackhammer."

He lowered his eyes. "Her case is getting to me more than she is. It seems like everything I come up with is either bad news or further confuses an already confusing situation. I've never had a case like this. I'm not even sure what to think anymore."

Amber held up the card. "Look carefully. The elephant's great weight should crush those fragile pots with their long narrow necks, right? But they show no distress and neither does the elephant. Neither of them is cracking. As long as nothing upsets the balance between them everything will be okay." She placed the card on the table. "You can handle the case. Just keep things in balance. You need to chill out. You probably feel like an elephant is sitting on you."

"I wish I knew how to chill out." He sighed.

"You can obtain pot legally now. And I don't mean like the ones on the card."

Early grinned. "Maybe Tikki can score for me. Or Hal can snag some from the evidence locker."

"Promoting juvenile crime and suborning police corruption? I never knew you were such a badass."

"As if I would be involved in any of that fun stuff. But how does this card help me figure out who the dark-haired woman is? We're still stuck with the problem that Siri is blonde."

Amber shrugged. "Perhaps the woman isn't Siri. Are other women involved in the case?"

Early gnawed on his knuckle for a moment. "I did see a dark-haired woman at the Hammond mansion. I don't know who she is or how important she might be, but I'm sure she's hiding something. Everybody connected to Chandler Hammond is."

"Sounds like one hot mess. And you right in the middle, huh?"

"Getting hotter and messier all the time." He stood up. "I can't wait to see what kind of hot mess turns up when I search the Hammond family camp tomorrow."

"Don't run into Sasquatch." Amber returned the deck to the drawer and picked up her feather duster.

"He'd be scared of me." Early laughed as he walked out the door. "My feet's too big."

15

IN WHICH BEGINS AN EARLY HUNTING TRIP

Early's butt bounced around on his spacious bench seat. The Caprice was scrupulous about hitting every pothole on the long and winding dirt road to the Hammond family camp. Even bicyclists couldn't avoid the numerous potholes and deep ruts during mud season. Speedy trips were something Mainers only dreamed of.

He hoped Honoria's directions were good. Along with the chattering of both his teeth and the car, there was always the possibility of being on the wrong road. Even his GPS gave him bad directions now and then. To be on the safe side he recited the Maine driver's prayer: "Lead me not into the sandy shoulder or deep ditch, amen."

Something approximating a driveway came into view. He checked Honoria's map and saw he was near an X she had made. During his career, he had been in some of Maine's most remote spots, and this was one of them. As he drove along, the driveway started looking more like a cow path on steroids and became even narrower than the dirt road he'd just left. Sticker bushes scraped against his doors.

Small boulders, more ruts, and large water-filled depressions made the drive an adventure.

Early shook his head. Someday he'd buy a proper Maine pickup truck with four-wheel drive and decent ground clearance. Regardless of the beefed-up suspension on his former cop car, he was uneasy about driving on such a waffle iron. He decided walking would be better.

Honoria had estimated the driveway as about a mile long. He hoped she was as bad at distances as she was good at directions; then, he realized this could cut both ways— the driveway might be shorter, but it might be longer. He stopped hoping and started hiking.

Halfway up he paused to take a whizz. During shoulder season, Maine was empty enough for the entire woods to be his bathroom. He glanced around to ensure he wasn't sharing the facilities, took aim at a dragonfly sitting on a leaf, and missed. "Usta could hit those," he muttered, zipping up.

The cabin was around the next bend. Grateful, Early perched on a log and waited for his breath to catch up to him. He pulled out a stick of nicotine gum and slipped the wrapper into his pocket. Leave no trace. Good advice for criminals too. Was this cabin a crime scene? Had Hammond been murdered here? *Oh hell, I don't even know if the guy's dead.*

Mottled sunlight shone through the trees on its way to the forest floor. This remote wilderness was so hushed that people could hear their hearts talk. Early's heart started to talk about the long-legged bronze beauty he had married.

Spring moves a man's blood and such moments held emotional danger. He wondered for the hundredth time why his wife had left. Did he say or do something wrong? Or not say or do something right? That line about finding her True Essence seemed bogus. And why leave Tikki?

Only birds and bugs observed him as he remembered the secluded place he and his bride had stumbled upon during their honeymoon in Baxter State Park. It was just like this place—elegant evergreens, shining birches, clear blue sky, and the pine scent of the deep woods. They had made love on the soft brown earth. Now he could almost feel her touch on his shoulders again, his skin tingling as her long fingernails glided down his back . . .

He shivered. Why had she deserted their private paradise abruptly? He never saw it coming. *Some detective I am.*

Early had handled plenty of divorce cases where obvious warning signs were missed. Even when they weren't, denial could be overpowering. A guy would say he just wanted to make the woman happy, ignoring her efforts to get away. Was he that guy?

And in the darkness at the back of his mind, he still couldn't shake the feeling that she had left him for another man. Melancholy as sad as a coyote's midnight howl descended upon him.

He tried to distract himself by appreciating the nice weather. It was a glorious sunny day, with enough blue sky to make a pair of Dutchman's pants. Soon crocus would sprout and the aroma of honeysuckle would fill the air.

It didn't work. He still sat on the pity pot. His old familiar depression had followed him to this beautiful place like a black cloud on a tether.

He took a lungful of clean forest air. The piney smell relaxed him somewhat, but he still felt like a hole had been ripped in his spirit. Early didn't dull his pain with booze or drugs—he tried to deal with it by immersing himself in his work. *What work?* How could he immerse himself in an eyedropper?

Wait, work was why he was here. Better start immersing. He stretched forward, his gaze dropping to the forest floor, idly following a small brown snake as it slithered across some footprints.

Hunting season was always open on something or other in the Maine woods and seeing human tracks wasn't unusual. But hunters didn't leave spike-heeled footprints. Early jumped up and followed the prints to where they met some tire tracks. *Siri's big black rockhopper can easily get up here. I wonder if these are her footprints.*

The prints led from the tire tracks to the cabin and back. Early had seen no vehicle but proceeded with caution anyway. The prints didn't look very old; someone could be here—maybe a dead someone. He crept over to the cabin and peered through a window.

The inside was dim but neat and tidy. No dead body in sight.

Were the footprints Honoria's? He had seen her only in slippers but thought she could be a spike-heel kind of woman. He pulled out his phone. No signal. *That's why Maine camps are where they are.*

The cabin was unlocked, not unusual way out here. He flipped the light switch and the gas lamps slowly brightened to reveal a great room and bedroom. Pretty fancy camp—in the North Woods a two-room cabin was practically a castle. The place looked cozy and comfortable, with no trace of mayhem.

The door slammed behind him followed by the sound of running footsteps.

Early dashed outside and saw a small long-haired figure

disappearing into the trees. Was it Siri? But she had no reason to run from him. Then it hit him: *Taziz.*

He gave chase, forgetting his exhaustion. He knew his feet wouldn't fail him but wasn't sure about his lungs. *I'm glad I gave up smoking.*

The fugitive tried to hide but wasn't very good at it— Early glimpsed a tuft of hair quivering behind a huge log. He bent over and panted loudly to feign exhaustion, hoping whoever it was would be fooled into feeling safe enough to bolt.

The plan worked. She sprang from behind the log and scampered through the forest like a rabbit. Early could barely discern asses and elbows, as his service buddies used to say, with long hair streaming out behind her. At last here was his dark-haired woman.

Early dashed through the woods, his long legs gaining ground on the fugitive. He got within leaping range and took her down with a flying tackle. She kicked like a Missouri mule as he pressed her face against the ground to subdue her. This time he managed to dodge flailing elbows and feet.

He got a solid enough grip to slap on the cuffs; then, he stood up and pulled his captive to her feet. His captive took the opportunity to kick him in the shin, yank her arm away, and sprint off. "Damn," Early yelled. "Why do I have such trouble hanging onto women?"

He watched her vanish into the woods, surprisingly fast for somebody in handcuffs. This wasn't going to be easy. He dodged trees in hot pursuit, getting close enough to grab her arm. She spun around, thrashing and screaming, "Let me go, let me go," eyes big as soccer balls.

Early froze. "Who the hell are you?"

Taziz it wasn't. Struggling in the detective's sizeable mitt was a boy barely older than Tikki.

"My—my name is Carly," the kid said, squirming. "Who are you?"

Early managed to pull out his ID. "James Early of the Early Detection Agency. What are you doing here?" He didn't think the kid was a Hammond. "Are you here with your family?"

The boy straightened up, scowled, and spit on the ground. "Hell no, I hope none of them are anywhere near here."

"That answers my question. You're a runaway."

The boy stared at the ground in sullen silence.

"And your name's not really Carly, is it?"

"No, sir," the kid said, simmering down a bit.

"Then, what is it?"

"I'm not telling ya. Yer gonna call Child and Family Services and they'll send me back. To *them.*"

He began to cry.

Early was unsure what to do. Because his son wasn't a crier, he didn't have much experience with sobbing children. But more than one betrayed spouse had cried on his broad shoulder and he figured a good cry was a good cry no matter what the cause. He placed a hand on the kid's quivering back.

"Look, son. We don't have to call anybody right now. I'm here to investigate a disappearance, not to track you down. Just tell me your real name."

The boy shuddered. Early removed the handcuffs to let him wipe his tears. "My real name is George."

"Hi, George. Call me Early." He took out his nicotine gum and offered some to George, who took a stick. "Why did you run away?"

"My mom found out . . ." He wavered.

"Kid, I've been a private investigator for a few decades and, before that, I was in the Air Force. Believe me, I've seen just about everything."

George laughed. "What the hey?"

"Okay, maybe not everything yet. What I'm saying is no matter how bad things seem you can talk to me. I have lots of listening experience."

"I ran away because . . ." George started sniffling again and said in a fast, harsh whisper, "my mom found out that I —I'm gay."

"That's all? I thought maybe you murdered somebody."

"She acted like I did."

"How'd she find out?"

"A little shit in school narced on me."

"Watch your mouth, young man," Early said automatically. "Things might have gone better if your mom had heard it from you instead."

"Maybe. I just wish . . ." He sighed and stared into the distance.

"She'll get over it. Or maybe not. Doesn't matter. You can't unring that bell now."

"Jeezum crow, you sure can't."

"Watch your mouth, young man."

"That ain't hardly cussing sir. I'm jest spleeny right now. I didn't expect you would catch me." George rubbed his wrists.

Early smiled. "Let's go back to the cabin. Maybe you can help with my investigation."

"I'll help. What are you investigating?"

"I'm trying to find the owner of that camp where you were hiding. He disappeared a while ago."

"Who's cunnin' little camp is that? I hid there because I was too tired to walk any farther yesterday."

"It belongs to Chandler Hammond."

"Chandler Hammond? Wait, isn't he some rich guy who ran off with his girlfriend?"

Early face-palmed. He couldn't believe he was hearing this in the middle of the North Woods. Some kinds of word got around way too fast in Maine.

16

IN WHICH EARLY FINDS A HUNKA-HUNKA BURNIN' LOVE

E arly walked George back to the cabin. *I hope this kid didn't contaminate the scene. My investigation still needs some meat on the bone and a bone is all I have. If there's nothing useful here I've struck out again.*

Inside, Early checked in and under a rustic chair, and then said, "Sit tight here, George. Do you live close by?"

George flopped down. "Yonder in Castle Rock."

"Quite a hike for a kid in moccasins. No wonder I didn't see your footprints. Maybe you should be a Maine Guide."

George grinned. "I thought about it. Or a game warden."

"You shouldn't be hiking all alone."

"I do it a lot. Got some Penobscot in me."

"That may be true, but you should always let somebody know where you expect to be. It's way too easy to get lost."

"Well, you know where I am."

"But your mom must be worried."

George fingered a shiny gray button on his red flannel shirt. "She doesn't care. She hates me for being gay. She's probably glad I'm gone—if she even noticed. My mom's usually too drunk to care about anything."

"I'm sure your mom doesn't really hate you. What about your dad?"

"My dad's in jail."

"Why's your dad in jail?"

"He shot the neighbor."

"Say what? Why?"

George settled back in his chair. "He owed the neighbor money for painting his Harley."

"Did the neighbor threaten him? Like pay up or else?"

"No, sir. He just come over and asked for his money. I guess Dad didn't have it, so he shot him. Sometimes my folks are number than a hammered thumb."

"Yeah, why not stab the neighbor? Bullets are expensive."

"I guess because my dad was on drugs."

That explained things. George's father had probably spent all his money on drugs. Early was familiar with substance abuse in rural Maine as well as its effects on kids caught in the middle. "What about you? Do you drink? Got any drugs on you?"

George's jaw dropped. "I would never! Not after I seen what it done to my mom and dad."

Early wondered if there was any liquor in the camp. If George was lying, Early didn't want the kid getting shitfaced on his watch. He checked the few cabinets for alcohol but to his relief found none. Liquor didn't last long in a rustic camp anyway.

Early eyed George. "You seem about my son's age."

"I'll be sixteen in a few weeks."

"Okay, we'll decide what to do about you after I finish my investigation."

"Cool. Can I watch?"

"Neither of us has much choice." Early sniffed the air.

"You a hound-dawg now?"

"I'm checking for a dead-body smell."

"You think somebody slipped their wind in here?" George looked around and shuddered. "Gross!"

"Huh? Don't you kids see worse these days? TV, video games, the internet . . ."

"I know what a dead body smells like—bad."

Early wondered if he had stumbled across a human bloodhound. "Smell anything like that in here?"

George inhaled deeply. "No, sir."

"Nor do I. Either nobody is dead or they're too dead to stink." He pulled out his phone and set it on a nearby table to record his examination of the sparse furniture—bunk beds, tables and upholstered chairs, bureau, meager kitchen cabinets, and wastebaskets. He even checked the attached outhouse but found nothing. He grabbed his phone to head outside but the sight of a cell phone on a small table beside the front door stopped him.

Was this Hammond's phone? Early ached to check out its contents but didn't want to contaminate possible evidence. He scooped it into a plastic bag and placed it into his pocket, then stepped outside to video the yard. Sometimes people threw trash into the woods rather than pack it up or burn it and trash was good for leads.

Burning? Wait, I need to check the best trash disposal of all: the fireplace.

Grasping his phone, he walked back inside the cabin and knelt next to the stone-faced hearth to feel the ashes. They were cold. "Are these your ashes?"

"No, sir. Maybe they're from the person who was here?"

Early's head snapped around. "Somebody else was here?"

"Yes, sir."

"What did they look like?"

"Well . . . I didn't see a *person*."

Early rolled his eyes. "What did you see, an alien?"

"I saw one of them big black SUVs drive out the dooryard."

"Did you see the driver?"

"No, sir. It had them dark windows."

I was right, Siri's car was here. But who was driving? The same person Jeremy said he couldn't see?

"I was some tired," George said, "and after the SUV left, I set my bedroll on the floor and went to sleep. This morning I ate a candy bar for breakfast. Then you showed up. I never had a chance to start no fire."

"Good thing. You might have disturbed a potential crime scene."

"Like CSI?" George bounced in his chair.

Kids. Investigations seem glamorous to them. I wonder what they'd make of the times I've had to squeeze into crawlspaces and under skanky old trailers with bugs and mud and who knows what other stinking crap was down there.

When he picked up a poker to stir the ashes a charred piece of paper popped out onto the floor. He picked it up by its burnt edges.

George leaned forward. "Is it a clue?"

"Maybe. Seems to be part of a letter. I can just barely make out the handwriting." He began reading aloud.

My dearest love. I am sorry to flee, but I fear for my life. I took [illegible] from the safe and returned to the cabin as you told me, but I cannot hide here forever. Nor can I face the possibility of living the rest of my life in a prison for what has happened. Tomorrow I will leave America for [burn hole]. Please do not search for me. Our time together was good and I swear I will never forget but now is the end. I wish for you the best of success in your plan to

The letter ended in a jagged rip.

"Touching," Early mumbled. "I wonder who wrote this." He suspected Hammond until he remembered that the only footprints he had seen here were from spike-heeled shoes. Hammond may be the devil, but he probably didn't wear Prada.

Maybe Hammond wrote the letter and its recipient brought it here with her? But would that be Siri or Taziz? Or was the letter written to him? Maybe it was from the woman on Taziz's flash drive—he still didn't know who she was. And why burn it?

Was someone else involved in this case, a person yet unknown to him? Siri didn't care about her husband's girl-friend because she had her own girlfriend . . . or was there more than one?

He blew some ashes off the letter and reread it. Who had been "hiding" at this camp and what "plan" did they wish someone success in?

"Did you see anything or anyone around here besides the black SUV?" Early asked.

"No, sir."

The letter was a substantial if confusing clue. He stuffed it into a plastic evidence envelope and dropped it into his other pocket. "Stay put while I finish searching the outside."

"Can't I watch some more?"

"Tell you what: see if you can find any other footprints in the driveway."

"On it." George jumped up and dashed out the door.

Early returned to videoing his slow and meticulous search. He was in no hurry to hike back down that hellacious driveway.

George returned with his report. "No tracks besides the ones you said you already seen. I did find some was made by Sasquatch about size thirteen." He checked out Early's shoes.

"Wise ass," Early growled, turning off his phone. He figured the letter, the footprints, and the tire tracks were the only relevant things to be found here. "Leave no trace," he murmured. To Early's frustration, the cabin's most recent inhabitant had possessed a commendable ecological conscientiousness.

They went back inside. "Pick up your stuff and let's get going."

"Where?" George shrieked, startling Early. "Are you taking me back to *them*?"

Early placed his hand on George's shoulder. "Calm down, kid. You're coming home with me until we sort things out. But you do realize we'll have to contact your folks at some point."

"I guess." George grabbed his bedroll and slouched out the door.

Early switched the lights off, closed the door, and took a last look around. A sudden thought struck him—Amber had seen a cabin in the woods and, sure enough, here it was.

Early recalled reading that over a third of police departments in the fifty largest American cities had consulted psychics and found them unhelpful. They could provide corroboration like seeing a corpse near water, but if a body were found in that location later it was usually the result of plain old police work. Cops considered psychics too vague to be useful.

"Hey, Early, you coming?"

"Shh, I'm thinking." Years ago, a friend of Amber's had had a recurring vision of a star on a road map where she felt a missing girl's body would be located. At the time the girl wasn't considered dead and she had no connection to the woman. The woman wasn't a psychic, and she hadn't offered to help the police. But a few months later the girl's body was found exactly where the map's star had indicated it would be . . . a thousand miles from where she had vanished.

How did Amber's friend know? Would psychic visions be helpful if they were better controlled? Maybe someday we'll find out.

"Early"—George hopped down the driveway around the rocks and ruts—"keep up!"

Early shuffled his sore feet down the driveway. A dense darkness had crept into the woods and he wanted to get home before nightfall. On the long, rocky, muddy slog to his car, he realized he had read that police study on psychics over twenty years ago. "Psychics are as over as pet rocks—now the internet knows everything," he mumbled as he stumbled.

17

IN WHICH HIPPOS AREN'T THE ONLY
HUNGRY HUNGRY CREATURES

The light of dawn seared Early's bleary eyes. Many Mainers were already halfway through their workday. Usually, he wasn't one of them, but he wanted to tell Hal about Hammond's Ponzi scheme while the morning was calm. He expected the Chief to ream him for committing burglary. Early liked to keep Hal in the dark about such things to give him plausible deniability, but this case had grown too big.

On Hal's porch, he jumped aside as the Chief's son, Darren, dashed by in pursuit of the school bus. "Morning, Uncle Early. Sorry."

"Zat you, Early? Come on in," Hal called from his sunny, warm kitchen.

Early found him sitting at the breakfast table like Jabba the Hutt, stuffing his face and listening to the radio. "Want some eggs? Martha makes the best omelet in Finderne."

"I'll just have a cuppa, thanks." Early sat down. The Chief's corgi ambled up and placed her paw on his foot, big brown eyes begging him to have mercy on her empty stomach. He reached down to scratch her. "Hi, Hungry."

"Hungry, shoo," Hal said, waving the dog off with his fork.

"Shoo? As if." Early laughed.

Hungry closed her eyes and smiled, enjoying the attention. Convinced that Early had no food, she lay down underneath the table to wait until he did.

"The dog's no bother, but puh-leeze turn off that damn shit-kicking music."

Hal rose and poured a cup of coffee. "Country music is good. 'As I drove out onto the street of this dirty little town . . .'" he warbled.

"That's *walked* out."

"Not these days." Hal turned down the radio and returned to his chair, handing Early the coffee.

"It's more like 'Waaaalll muh mama got drunk and muh daddy got drunk . . .'" Early twanged.

"Freeze," yelled the Chief.

"No," Early shouted. "'And muh dawg got drunk and muh hoss got drunk . . .'"

"Don't make me throw you into the slammer," the Chief growled, pointing his fork.

Early raised his hands. "I surrender officer. Sorry, but country music was all I ever heard on guard duty. Sometimes I was so bored I thought I'd have to prop my eyelids open with toothpicks."

"Sounds painful." Hal flashed a big grin and shoveled a forkful of eggs into it. "Where's the fire this morning? Or is it just smoke again?"

"Stop poking fun at me or I'll sue for false arrest. Jeremy has a big mouth."

"He does." Hal snickered. "I'm just wondering what's important enough to get even you out of bed at this hour."

Early wasn't quite ready to confess. He developed an

intense interest in the floor and thought of pulling out a bullet to bite. Hal would laugh at that until he heard about the burglary. He decided to ease into things by retrieving the tooth from his pocket and placing it on the table.

Hal poked the tooth with his fork as if it were a dead bug. "What the hell is this?"

"A tooth I found in Siri's pottery ashes yesterday."

"And you're showing me this because you think it's not from an animal?"

"Looks human to me," Early said.

"Maybe but we didn't go to dental school. Did you ask her about it?"

"No. I wanted you to see it first. I think it could be Hammond's tooth."

"Great Hitchens' ghost." Hal scrutinized the tooth as if he expected to find a name engraved on it.

"Siri almost fainted when she saw me checking out an empty cooler by her kiln shed."

"Early, make sense for once. Why would Siri faint if she caught you snooping around? She should be used to it by now."

Early bit his lip. "I'll get to that. But don't you read true-crime stories? A loose tooth turning up where a missing person was last seen is suspicious."

Hal grinned. "I *am* a true-crime story. But how can you prove this is Hammond's? We don't have his DNA and even his dentist wouldn't be able to ID one tooth. Hell, is this thing even real?"

"There's more. I found this letter fragment and cell phone near the fireplace of the family's mountain camp." He pulled out the plastic evidence bags and handed them to the Chief.

Hal scrutinized the phone. "You think this is Hammond's?"

"Or somebody close to him. Why else would it be there?"

The Chief began reading the letter through the plastic bag. "Strange. 'I swear I will never forget but now is the end'? Sounds like a cheap romance novel."

"You read those things?"

"The girls leave them lying around the house. I'll pick one up when I need a laugh."

Early chuckled. "What do you make of that letter? Could it be evidence?"

"Of what? We haven't received any recent reports about missing safe contents down at the station."

That surprised Early. Why hadn't Siri called the cops when she discovered the money was gone? He was sure the mystery woman had taken it, and Siri had to know by now.

"But if the writer burned this instead of mailing it, the victim might still be unaware that anything's missing," Hal said.

"Finding that letter in the cabin narrows down the pool of robbery victims."

"To either Siri, Hammond, or Honoria."

"Or Taziz," Early said.

"You interrupted my peaceful breakfast for this? An unidentified tooth, an orphaned cell phone, and a half-burned letter? You know this isn't a police matter anymore, right? We closed the case."

"One more thing. A runaway boy was hiding out at the cabin."

"Is he a minor? We'll have to call Child and Family Services," Hal said.

"He goes ballistic whenever I mention doing that. He thinks they'll send him back to his mom."

"The agency will consider whether he's old enough to choose where he wants to live. Is he still up there?"

"No, he's at my house with Tikki."

"Bring him by the station later and we'll sort things out." Hal leaned in and folded his hands. "You remember those child deaths in the midcoast last year. I know he's an older kid and can take care of himself but . . ."

Early lowered his head. "But we don't know what his family situation is. Most of the shootings in Maine every year are due to domestic violence. I would hate to think we're sending him back to something like that."

Hal checked his phone file. "I can get him into a residential program, but it might take a while."

"He can stay with me until you find one."

"You know he'll age out of the system in a few years."

Early smiled. "We'll cross that bridge when we come to it."

Hal sat back. "Speaking of crossing bridges, remember that jogger in the Santa suit you saw a while ago? You'll never believe what happened last night at the quickie mart down by the bridge on Broadway—"

The Chief's words drowned in a cacophony of giggling as a torrent of golden-skinned girls burst through the kitchen door. "Uncle Early," they screamed in unison. "Wassup?"

Early laughed as Hal's three daughters smothered him in hugs. "Your Dad and I are discussing a case."

"About what?" one girl asked, pulling open the refrigerator door to peer inside.

"Now sweetie, you know your Uncle Early and I are not allowed to talk about open cases," Hal admonished.

"Oh poo." She pouted, hands on hips. "Then, tell me where the toaster pastries are."

"On the counter, honey, next to the toaster."

"Those are mine, hands off," another daughter shouted, igniting a deluge of yelling about who was entitled to eat what.

Early felt a growing appreciation for his quiet and sensible son. "Great Hitchens' ghost, Hal. Are mornings always like this?"

"Sometimes worse. Boys may be boisterous but girls are loud. I'm usually gone before they get up. You can see why." Hal rose, walked to the kitchen door, and looked down the hall.

Bemused, Early followed. "Isn't this the whole crew? You expecting somebody else?"

Hal glanced back into the kitchen. "One, two, three. You're right, they're all here." He laughed. "I was hoping Martha would come to help me lay down the law, but she must have hit the Jacuzzi." He sighed and turned back to the feminine mob. "Listen up, girls."

The girls whined. Hungry barked. Hal rumbled. "Here's some reality, kids: the person with the most seniority gets the most stuff. Remember that, it will serve you well in life."

Amused and unenvious, Early watched Hal portion out the toaster pastries according to age. Hungry barked to remind everyone of their duty to drop crumbs.

"Bust a move, girls, or you'll be late for school," the Chief said.

"Already are," they chirped altogether, sloshing a jug of orange juice each of them was trying to grab.

Hal turned back to Early. "Quick, follow me to my nice quiet study." He set a brisk pace across the hall with Early hard on his heels, both glad to escape the pandemonium.

18

IN WHICH THERE ARE TRUE CONFESSIONS

Hal flopped into the well-worn brown leather chair at his large mahogany desk and fingered the bagged cell phone. "I'll get one of my detectives to match the contents of this with Hammond's records. That will tell us if this is his phone."

"Easier than contacting the service provider." Early chuckled as he pulled out Hammond's flash drive. "This contains all of Crystalline's corporate records."

"Siri gave you that?"

"Not really."

Early saw the Chief's cop radar emerge. He gripped the arms of his chair to keep from squirming. *Here it comes.*

Hal thrust a finger into his face. "Early, what have you been up to? Someday you're going to land in a steaming pile of feces and I won't be able to dig you out."

"You always tell me to wipe that shit-eating grin off my face," Early said through his shit-eating grin.

The Chief slapped his palm against the desktop. "That's it. I don't want to know any more details of your investigation."

"Don't worry about that. But you need to see the list of Crystalline's investors on here."

"Wait . . . Hammond had to keep a *list*? I thought he was pulling in just us local folks."

"He was. Maybe he had a bad memory. Anyway, funny money is a good reason to disappear. It could explain Hammond's sudden departure."

Hal looked at the flash drive. "Hammond has lived here for many years and has ties to the community; he's a country club member and he was president of the Chamber of Commerce. But if he was into something shady that would be a good reason to reopen the case. I think you had better tell me where you got this."

Early hung his head and mumbled, "I stole the original from Hammond's safe and Tikki made this copy."

"You could have come to me for a search warrant."

"A search warrant for what? I only suspected Hammond might be going broke. I didn't know what he was really up to until I saw the company files. Have the police ever gotten any calls from Crystalline's investors?"

"Not that I recall. Should we have?" Hal asked.

"Plug this into your laptop and see."

Hal inserted the drive into the laptop on his desk and pulled up a list of files. "Yeah, so?"

"You don't see anything strange?"

"Circus Tickets? Company Picnic? Looks like personal stuff," Hal said.

"Why the hell would Hammond keep a file on circus tickets he bought?"

"You're trying to make something out of nothing. Maybe he gave them to investors. They'd be a tax-deductible business expense."

"Then you'd think his taxes would be on here too," Early said.

"They would have to be. Financial business programs integrate all that stuff."

"There's no financial program on there, and no tax forms either. Open one of the files."

"I like clowns. How about Circus Tickets?" The Chief opened the file, blinked, and said, "This looks like his list of investors. Why would he call it 'Circus Tickets'?"

"Seems Hammond thinks he can cover his ass by giving his files fake names. Crystalline's really a Ponzi scheme. It's a fake company and there is no money."

Hal turned nearly as white as his name. "No!"

"My smart son was able to figure that out even without the COFEE program you gave him," Early said with a smirk.

The Chief lowered his eyes. "Tikki told you about that, eh?"

"We didn't even need to use it. The files are in plain sight."

"Okay, I'll ignore your means of obtaining this drive if you give me a pass on letting Tikki have the COFEE program."

"Done." Early could hope for no better plea bargain. "Corroborating evidence: according to the financial reports on that drive Crystalline posted dividends and sent out reports to only four investors."

"Accounting and documentation requirements for corporate investing are very strict." Hal shook his head. "If you're right, it looks like Hammond was trying to avoid a paper trail. We've got enough red flags here to stop a NASCAR race."

"And Honoria is in the lineup."

The Chief turned to Early. "He scammed his own sister?"

"At least that proves she wasn't in on the fraud."

"Being a victim is clearing yourself the hard way. Hammond sent out only four financial reports?"

"You can see them on that drive. And they only went to the names on the list where a dividend was noted," Early said.

"I see—nondisclosure let him avoid explaining how a local art distributorship could be worth what he claimed it was. He was free to make up any figure he liked."

"Why would all those people trust his word?"

"You and I have seen how greed can cause people to disregard the most obvious warning signs." Hal tented his fingers. "Hammond probably doesn't see his investors much. And I can just imagine what goes on when he does: haha old pal, slap on back, yes, Crystalline is doing just great. Gotta run, see ya."

"There's something else. Tikki found a mysterious letter from Hammond to a guy by the name of Larry Bloch, who Honoria told me is a college friend of his who sells real estate in the Boston area. I think we need to find out when he saw Hammond last and what he knows about Crystalline—"

There was a knock on the doorway and a tall, blonde woman walked into the room. "Hi Early." She bent over to kiss Hal's bald head. "Hope I'm not interrupting."

"Your interruptions are always welcome, babe," Hal said, holding her hand. "What's on your mind, Martha?"

"I thought I heard you mention Crystalline."

Hal tilted his head. "That interested you?"

"I meant to tell you that Chandler Hammond gave a talk to my garden club last month. He said Crystalline would be a good investment for us. We decided to buy in because we liked the name of the company."

The smile on Hal's face froze like Maine in January.

Early stepped up when he saw the Chief was stricken. "How much did your club invest?"

"A few hundred dollars."

Early and Hal both exhaled. "We can discuss this later, babe."

"Sure. Now that the kids have left for school, I can have a nice quiet breakfast." She turned and walked out.

"Early, didn't you see the garden club's name on the list?" Hal hissed.

"No. Maybe I thought it was somebody named Garden Club."

"Dammit, he scammed my wife. I'm gonna nail that son of a bitch," the Chief snarled. "Shit, we've gotta call in the feds. I welcome their help, but that can lead to media coverage. And the internet is the best way to spread anything by word of screen."

"Hey, if you want click bait, check out this flash drive I found in Taziz's apartment." Early pulled out the other drive.

"Don't tell me you stole that too?"

"Relax, J. Edgar. I had permission to search from her landlady gun-totin' Mrs. Leary." He handed the drive to the Chief.

"What's on here?"

"Let's just say you shouldn't let your kids catch you looking at it."

"You mean . . . porn?"

"Porn is in the eye of the beholder. What you'll behold is Siri and another woman getting busy."

Hal grinned. "I'd better view this at the station."

"Make sure your office door is locked or you'll have a crowd."

"Oh, you wouldn't believe the stuff we get in down there." Hal turned the flash drive over in his hand. "Siri had a girlfriend, too, huh? Would that be reason enough for her to knock off Hammond?"

"Women have killed their husbands for less."

"Maybe Hammond was planning to ditch his Ponzi scheme and move into something more legitimate like porn." Hal snickered. "Porn as a preferable business alternative to investment fraud. I love it." He turned back to his laptop screen and scowled. "Damn. Help me out here. How can we—"

"What you mean we?"

Hal looked around to catch Early's own vanishing act. Out the door.

19

IN WHICH EARLY TUMBLES INTO A STINKING PIT OF MISERY

Tikki was still in school and George was at the police station helping Hal find a suitable residential program, giving Early sole access to the family laptop. In order to prove Crystalline was not a legitimate company, he needed to find comparative financial data on raku pottery: sales volume, who the buyers were, anything that would help him contrast Crystalline's meager revenue with the market data.

He tossed his coat onto the couch, burying the cat. She jumped to the floor, shooting him a look of green-eyed disapproval for his disrespect. Early laughed. Cats always outclassed humans when it came to scathing looks. "Sorry to disturb, your Catness."

"Mrrwowrr," the cat said, stiffening her tail like a mast as she marched into the spare room. Early trailed after her and sat down at the laptop.

He spent the next hour basking in the silvery light of the internet but found nothing to substantiate Crystalline's alleged fat bottom line. Raku was expensive and pieces from internationally acclaimed artists could run to five figures. But millions? That kind of money was never on the table and, despite her bragging, Siri was no high-priced superstar. Crystalline would have had to fill every pot with drugs to pull in the kind of revenue Hammond claimed the company had.

Although the contraband idea wasn't original, Early had seen no signs of smuggling. The pottery market's online revenue figures only confirmed what he and Tikki suspected: Hammond was building his fortune on investors, not inventory.

Early leaned back to contemplate the fine plaster cracks in the ceiling. Had only four of Crystalline's investors been blessed with the sense to request a balance sheet before giving up their money? Hammond seemed to reel in suckers with nothing but a good line of bullshit. This was not as preposterous as it seemed—possibly someone could even become President of the United States on the strength of that some day.

Without documentation, the financier could lie his ass off. Waving a high return in front of potential investors was probably the easiest way to convert them into true believers. As far as Early could tell, the company had no prospectus, no annual reports, and not even a website. But since investors were mostly financial investment newbies, this apparently had not raised any suspicions. Maybe the investors even swept in their friends and families like Hammond had.

The guy's nerve was as incredible as his luck. *What the hell is his charm and how can I get some?* Early pictured Hammond's marks slapping each other on the back for getting in on the ground floor and saying on the golf course, "Our fellow Chamber and country club member is trustworthy, right? He's one of us. Everybody knows him. He's okay."

Early was getting quite the education. Up until now, he wouldn't have believed that greed could be as blinding as love.

He was glad he had uncovered the Ponzi scheme, but the scam was becoming a distraction from his real assignment. None of the corporate information he unearthed had gotten him any closer to finding Hammond. Just the opposite— now that he had uncovered a crime, Early thought Hammond really was hiding out, making him even more difficult to locate.

Early didn't feel like he was seeing the big picture. Some cases had missing pieces like incomplete jigsaw puzzles, but this case was like a mashup of different puzzles—nothing seemed to fit. He needed more pieces of this puzzle. And there was still the possibility that Hammond would walk through the front door of his mansion tomorrow. Maybe Taziz would walk in with him. Or maybe both of them would be found floating in the Penobscot River. Nothing could be ruled out yet.

Trying to be less pessimistic, he grabbed the mouse and continued slogging through more data. The cat jumped onto the desk. "Hi anonymous kitty," he said, stroking her glossy fur. The little black cat purred and arched her back in glee. The sight helped Early relax and he noticed a link to a website he hadn't checked out yet, *Everything Raku*.

The colorful site was full of information about creating and collecting raku, but it contained no market data. He almost left, but, since the cat had already distracted him, he decided to take a break from finance before he fell asleep and risked a concussion from his head hitting the desk.

He surfed through several images of pottery from

renowned artists all over the globe. *Wait a minute, I wonder whether this website mentions using teeth as a glaze additive.* As he searched for some relevant data, he noticed that red pots like Siri's latest batch seemed to be fairly rare. He began scanning a promising-looking article:

Raku was the name of a sixteenth-century family who produced hand-formed pottery for the Japanese tea ceremony.

At first, he was disappointed to see that most of the material seemed to be historical data unrelated to his case. He scrolled to a section on glazes and how oxidation and reduction affected them. The information was highly technical and almost as boring as the financial research he had just ditched. He skipped to another section on something he was more familiar with—kilns.

And there he discovered an old Chinese raku legend.

Had serendipity guided him? Intrigued, he read and reread the ancient tale, drawn in by its twisted path.

The king demanded that the potter make more of the pots. But the frustrated potter could not reproduce his results.

A hazy idea began to take shape in Early's brain. Slowly it became less misty and more concrete. He remembered Amber's words: *the images that formed in the alchemist's mind.*

Pots and alchemy. His mind was in way over its head.

He remembered the cooler in Hammond's safe. He was convinced it was the same cooler he had seen by Siri's kiln shed. What had really been inside those plastic bags? If only he had had more time.

Suddenly, the hazy idea lurking in the darkened back of his mind slammed into his brightly lit consciousness with the force of an erupting volcano.

What if? What if Hammond hadn't taken off with his girlfriend? What if Honoria was right? What if Siri killed him and then . . .

Early stiffened in numb horror. If the idea that had just barged into his mind in such a violent manner was a real possibility, he knew where Chandler Hammond had to be.

20

IN WHICH EARLY CONSIDERS
EMULATING HAMMOND

N*o way, this is crazy,* he mentally screamed in an effort to shake off the intrusive thought. But the gruesome suspicion stuck to Early like napalm and burned almost as much.

Okay, it's all over, this case had now officially turned him into a whack job. He remembered the elephant standing on the pots and Amber's advice to chill out. But there was no chance of doing that now.

Early was no stranger to real-life gore. He had seen messy suicides, bar fights with knives and broken bottles, even a guy decapitated by a helicopter blade at Loring Air Force Base. The details in some of Hal's cop stories were even more gruesome. But nothing pinned the needle on the perversion meter like the possibility that had just hit him.

That kind of thing simply doesn't happen around here.

Early shuddered. Was Siri capable of doing what he imagined? Even an ice queen like her—or would that be fire queen? He slapped his cheeks hard but that didn't clear his mind of the horror. He arose and stalked around the room but the scary thoughts followed him.

He leaned against the window gazing at the cream-colored birches, the green lawns, the neat street under the bright blue sky filled with fluffy white clouds. The sound of neighborhood children at play drifted by on a gentle warm breeze. He saw the serene and cozy Maine town of Find-erne, a town where *that kind of thing simply doesn't happen.* Strong sunlight stung his eyes but didn't burn away his distress.

I've got to snap out of it. Snap out of it. I've got to . . .
Yeah right.

His crazy notion was like a brain worm, an obsession that wouldn't turn him loose. His mind started throbbing. The hair stood up on his arms. He really, really wanted a cigarette.

Early was glad this idea hadn't occurred to him at the library. They would have thrown him out—or worse—when they saw him raving in the stacks like a lunatic. He fought to stay rational but the ghastly thoughts smashed each meager attempt.

Now he realized he needed to proceed carefully. This new revelation had turned the circumstances of the case from murky to dangerous and misinterpreting any small detail could lead to a disastrous mistake.

Early retook his chair and scoured the internet for more information about the ancient raku legend. The tale was widespread in the art pottery community and all the versions he located varied only slightly. But nothing in any of them dispelled the demented scheme that had infected his brain.

"Damn," he mumbled. "Raku can be brutal."

Still resisting his suspicions, he checked out the pottery galleries on the website of Siri's Seramics. He wanted his fears to be unfounded, deranged, even absurd—anything but possible.

No luck. What he saw only confirmed the depravity that had hijacked his mind.

Scrolling through her pictures made him almost want to scream. "How could I possibly consider something like this?" he whispered from a dry throat. "Would Siri be stupid enough to explain her entire artistic process to me if she had used it to . . ."

Uh yeah. Most criminals are pretty stupid. Especially first-time murderers.

The case had spun out of control, becoming more than a simple disappearance or a Ponzi scheme. And even worse: how could he possibly explain the bizarre theory he had just come up with to the Chief?

He hated that his research confirmed his idea, but would Hal see things that way too? This might be the case that convinced him that Early had finally lost it.

He needed to show Hal he had stumbled upon a major break in the case without being laughed out of the cop shop. That's what the police usually did to people with crazy theories and there was no shortage of folks in the tinfoil-hat brigade. Early never dreamed he would be one of those guys but sinister perceptions from the darker alcoves of his mind had now created an inextinguishable turmoil in his soul. Hal's feedback would be invaluable *if* the Chief believed him. The problem was to get Hal to consider a theory Early didn't want to believe himself even though he had come up with it.

"Great Hitchens' ghost," he moaned. "Why did I answer Honoria's phone call? Maybe Hal was right, I shouldn't have taken her case." He rubbed his face. "Maybe I can just disappear like Hammond did. Get the hell out, swear off private investigation, even re-up in the Air Force."

In the middle of this despair, he again heard his wife's voice when she told him she was leaving. Tikki's mother was gone and now his father wanted to run off too? The kid had had enough parental trauma drama to last him a lifetime. Early couldn't abandon his son and running away from a difficult situation would set a terrible example.

No. He had taken Honoria's case. He owed it to his client to stick by his word regardless of where the investigation led ... even into the cesspool where his mind had fallen.

He wiped his forehead and pulled out his phone to call Tikki, and then hesitated. Was it right to ask for his son's take on this? Regardless of what perversions existed in Tikki's video games, some real-life perversions shouldn't be run by a teenager.

He put the phone down. For once in his life, he felt truly alone. Maybe he should call Amber? *Nah, even someone as otherworldly as she is would have a hard time believing this.*

Bleary-eyed, dead tired, and greatly disturbed, he stared in numb exhaustion at Siri's pottery shining from the screen. The cheery colors stood in stark contrast to the dark and troubling scenario they now represented to him.

A loud slam broke his reverie and shattered his nerves. "Honey, I'm home."

Hearing Tikki's voice was just what he needed. Early returned almost to normal.

Tikki walked into the room, the cat scampering close behind him. Early jumped up and threw his arms around his son.

"Eeww, Dad, ick!" The kid tried to wriggle free but stopped squirming when he realized resistance was futile. Eventually, to his great relief, Early released him.

"You doing more research on Crystalline?" Tikki straightened his clothes in an effort to regain his cool and looked at the computer screen. "Nice pots."

Early frowned. "Yeah. Real nice." He wrestled the mouse from the cat and closed the browser. "Those are some of Siri Hammond's pots. I was gathering information on raku, but I'm done. Stick a fork in me. Now I know the real meaning of too much information."

21

IN WHICH THERE ARE FALSE
CONFESSIONS. OR NOT.

Early gave a mighty yank on the ornate front door of the Finderne police station's old Victorian mansion. Life was funny—in his youth, one of his top priorities had been to stay out of the cop shop, but now he was straining to get in.

After conquering the bulky door, he strolled across the squad room's creaky oak floor to the Chief's office. Hal was having a conversation with a young cop standing beside his desk.

"He mentions his new client, Harry Balzac, and his coworkers laugh," Hal said. "One of the secretaries says they don't have a client by that name. He tells her it's not his real name, nobody likes the guy, so they call him 'Harry Balzac' because that sounds like a certain part of a man's anatomy. She asks what part? Since she asked—and this is why she sued him—he says it sounds like hairy—oh, hi Early."

"You're sure getting a lot of mileage out of that 'wacky lawsuits' website we stumbled across. Sorry to interrupt, Richie." Early nodded to the young cop.

Richie probably wasn't sorry—every cop in Finderne

must have heard Hal's stories several times. The Chief was oblivious to their efforts to avoid a repeat and poor Richie was pretending to enjoy another retelling.

"You were pretty mysterious on the phone this morning," Early said.

"Have a seat. We'll pick this up later, Richie." He waved his hand and Richie scampered out the door.

Hal turned to Early. "You were right, that's Taziz in the pictures on the flash drive. I've seen her with Hammond at some of the Chamber meetings."

"He brought his girlfriend to them? What a set of brass balls. Or should I say Harry Balzac?"

Hal roared. "Wonder if Hammond knows about those pictures? I sent both drives to the evidence locker in case Taziz's drive turns out to be useful. But this is the real reason why I asked you here today." Hal tossed a small white envelope across his desk.

Early noted the return address. "You know somebody in Syria?"

"Apparently, I do now. Read it."

Early's jaw nearly hit the floor when he saw the signature. "It's from Taziz."

The Chief smiled. "And she sings like a little birdie."

Taziz, the exotic beauty who haunted Early at nearly every turn in the case. He imagined what her sultry voice must sound like as he began to read the neatly typed narrative.

That night Siri sent the staff on holiday and we made love beside the hearth of the great room. We thought Chandler was asleep in his room. I was kissing her navel when he came in to find us. He yelled what are you doing. I rose from the floor and said what does it look like Chandler. Then I told him Siri and I were in love.

"Nothing like blindsiding the guy," Early said.

"It gets better," the Chief said.

Early returned to the letter.

I licked my fingers. He became enraged and shouted you bitch. I don't know whether he meant me or Siri, but he repeated you bitch, you bitch. He said he hoped we bitches would be happy with each other and he is leaving. He turned away and walked down the hall to his office.

Siri got up and put on her robe. I tried to hold her back. I said let him go, let's finish. But she ran after him. I put on my clothes and pursued her to Chandler's office.

When I arrived, he was taking money from the safe and putting it into his briefcase. Siri tried to stop him. She hung onto his arm. I ran to help her. He punched me and kicked Siri across the room and she hit against the wall. He picked up his briefcase and walked out the back door toward the garage.

Siri crawled to Chandler's desk and took his gun out of the drawer. She ran outside after him and screamed for him to drop the money or she would shoot. I ran outside, but I couldn't see them in the dark. I heard angry voices, Chandler laugh, and a sound like someone being struck. There was a shot and another. Siri ran to me. She had his briefcase in her hand. She said the gun went off and Chandler is dead. I panicked and said what do we do? She told me to take the money from the briefcase and put it back in the safe.

"Nice," said Early. "Don't check to see if he's still breathing, just jump on the money. Those two were made for each other." Early continued reading.

> *I was putting money in the safe when Siri came in with a hatchet in her hand. She told me to go find trash bags in the kitchen for the disposing of Chandler's body. When I heard this, I vomited. I told her I want no part of this. She said everything was okay, she knew how to get rid of the body in such a way that it will never be found. She did not say how but she repeated one word over and over, it sounded like "kill." I think she was saying she killed Chandler. She wanted me to dispose of the gun, but I refused.*

"She's trying way too hard to convince us she had as little involvement as possible," Early said.

"Yes. Why else would she send this letter to the police?" He resumed reading.

> *Siri said she would dump the gun in the drink. I don't know what that meant. She told me to take her car and hide at the family cabin to look like Chandler and I had run away with the company money. She gave me his cell phone and told me to call her, so he would seem to be alive in case people asked questions. I drove her car to my flat and packed some things for my stay at the cabin. I don't know what happened at Chandler's house after I left.*

I hid in the cabin for several weeks. I had to drive Siri's car down from the cabin to call her. She told me never to speak to her and only leave blank messages. But I grew suspicious that she would dispose of me because I witnessed her murder Chandler. I decided the wisest thing for my safety was to flee the United States for home.

"She's saying Siri planned this whole disappearance story as a cover-up for murder," Early said.

"You think Taziz is telling the truth?"

"Who knows? Maybe Siri did kill her husband in a rage. Big money has unforeseeable effects on people. Maybe Taziz wrote the letter I found at the camp—if the letter was meant for Siri."

"Siri didn't write that letter. She didn't leave the country," the Chief said.

"She could have planted it though."

"Why would she plant anything?"

"To frame Taziz," Early said.

"Nobody tries to frame somebody else except the guilty."

"I rest my case." Early's chin rose.

"Even Siri could leave better evidence than that, maybe signing Taziz's name. I like Taziz for the camp letter, but we still don't know if it was for Siri or Hammond."

"If you believe the Syria letter, Hammond was already dead and couldn't have written or received the camp letter. That means Taziz must have written it to Siri," Early said.

"If she's lying about his death, she could have written it to Hammond or he could have written it."

"And if he did . . ."

"Then Taziz might have killed him to keep him from taking the money and leaving *her*. Read on," the Chief said.

Early's head was spinning with the idea that Taziz was the girlfriend of *both* Hammonds. What was she up to? Early went back to the letter.

I returned to the mansion on a night when I knew Siri to be gone. I took the money from the safe and went to the airport to purchase a ticket to Boston. I arrived in Boston and purchased an airplane ticket for France. From there I flew here to Syria where I feel safe. Soon I will return to my home in Iraq.

"She must be scared shitless of Siri if she feels safer in Syria."

"Safe from Siri in Syria," Hal murmured. "How poetic."

"Can we extradite her?"

"We have no idea where she is. All we know is that she was in Syria at some point. She might plan to stay there and said she's going back to Iraq as a red herring. If she's telling the truth about the robbery, she could have a few mil with her. That would go a long way in the Middle East." Hal drummed his fingers on the desk. "Truth is stranger than fiction but I'm not sure which one this letter is. Or which parts of it are what."

"This letter is to cover her ass, Hal. No way could Siri pull off a murder all by herself let alone dispose of the body," Early said.

"If Hammond is even dead. Hell, maybe *he* sent that letter from Syria as an elaborate ruse in order to get away with the cash. It's less transparent than a fake suicide."

"You mean the three of them cooked up this story to convince us that Hammond's dead? And nobody's up for a murder rap because there's no physical evidence?"

The Chief fixed a steely-eyed stare at him. "Don't you get it, man? Siri tried to make it look like Hammond absconded, but Taziz changed everything when she bolted. Now, Taziz wants us to think Siri murdered him to keep Siri from chasing her down to recover the money. The hilarious part is that Taziz thinks we're gonna take her word for it."

"We still don't know whether Hammond's alive or dead, murdered or not."

"Taziz does imply there's physical evidence," Hal said.

"A gun in the drink never to be found. A bloody hatchet —I'll bet it's sleeping with the gun, if either of them exists."

Hal sighed. "We don't know who's lying and who isn't."

"You could give Siri a polygraph."

"She'd probably refuse. Polygraphs aren't conclusive, anyway. The only fact we have is that Hammond is missing."

"And that Taziz and Siri were lovers. Those pictures prove it," Early said.

"Even if her story about Siri is true, positioning yourself as an accessory to murder is a stupid way to frame somebody."

Early tilted his head. "Does Siri know about this letter?"

"Not yet. I'm reopening the case and sending both letters to the lab. I'll wait until I receive their report to question her again. Unfortunately, there's no handwriting to compare since the Syria letter was typed."

Early's head reeled. He went over the letter again, trying to ferret out clues. "How did Siri know Hammond's Bentley was at the airport?"

"She said somebody called her to inquire about buying it because there was a 'For Sale' sign in the window. After she found out where it was, she had it towed back to the mansion."

"Why not sell the Bentley where it sat?" Early asked.

"She said she wasn't comfortable with leaving the car there. She showed us a towing receipt."

"Did you interview the tow truck driver?"

Hal frowned. "Another of Siri's dodges. There's no logo on the receipt and she couldn't remember the name of the towing company."

"Tikki and I spent a whole day viewing the airport parking lot security videos. We didn't see any Bentley. The head of parking told us he never heard of Chandler Hammond. I even showed him a picture of a Bentley, but he said he didn't recognize it. We checked for Siri's SUV too. Do you know how damn many black SUVs there must be in Maine? And I think they're all parked at the airport."

"You think Siri's towing receipt is bogus?"

"I do but there's no chance of finding out for sure. Even if she miraculously remembers the name of the towing service, I'm sure she greased the driver with a generous dose of hush money. Did she have a receipt for bailing the car outta the lot?" Early asked.

"No. She said Hammond had credit at the lot because he was there so frequently."

"So frequently the guy in charge never heard of him." Early snorted. "But what if Hammond never was at the airport? Maybe he and Taziz took off in the Bentley."

"And Siri chased them down and killed him to sell his car?" Hal chuckled. "That's one thing that checked out. We called the dealer she sold it to in California." The Chief leaned back. "I'll give you a call when Siri's interrogation video is ready for viewing."

Early noticed the Chief leering as he rose to leave. "Whassup?"

"Got an extra copy of Taziz's flash drive?"

"No, but Tikki will be glad to make one if we can borrow it back from the evidence room. And I'll be happy to deliver it to your wife personally."

22

IN WHICH THE INTERNET PROVES THAT IT REALLY DOES KNOW ALL

R ichie accompanied Early into the interrogation room where the Chief was powering up an old monitor.

"Where's the popcorn?" Early asked.

"Popcorn? You know police interrogations can make you woof your cookies," the Chief said.

"That's why I asked for popcorn instead of cookies. Was Siri's interrogation woofable?"

"Not as woofable as Taziz's letter."

The Chief hit play and Early watched as the interrogating detective placed the tooth from the ash can onto the table in front of Siri and asked, "Ever see this before?"

Siri recoiled as if the tooth were a live rattlesnake. "Ew, ick. What the hell is that?"

"You tell me," the interrogating detective said.

"What do you mean, I tell you? Obviously, it's a tooth. What am I supposed to tell you? Do I look like a damn dentist?"

"It's your husband's tooth found in the ashes from your kiln," the detective said.

"He's bluffing," Early cried.

"Yes," the Chief said. "We can't ID the tooth, but Siri doesn't know that. Listen to what she says."

"Oh," popped out of Siri's mouth in the phony squeak Early had come to know. "That's where it was? Chandler and I looked all over for that tooth." She smiled and drew a circle on the tabletop with her long crimson fingernail, murmuring, "I'm afraid I knocked it out when I punched him in the mouth."

Hal hit pause when he heard Early's facepalm. "Are you okay?"

"She punched him hard enough to knock a tooth out? And I thought she was cool and controlled."

"Sounds to me like she's just covering her ass. She offered up that explanation without even asking how we gained possession of the tooth. But by doing so she confirmed that it belonged to Hammond," Hal said.

"She didn't positively ID it. She can always recant and say she was mistaken."

"Sure, and teeth grow on lawns all over Finderne. Hammond's dentist told us he had some loose teeth due to gum disease and it's quite possible for one to be knocked out with a hard enough blow." Hal leaned back. "Hammond probably wouldn't tell his dentist that his wife punched him."

"Siri's not averse to wailing on people and she does pack quite a punch," Early said, rubbing his shoulder. "Did Hammond ever call the cops on her?"

Hal snorted. "I didn't check, but many men wouldn't. Times have changed, but many guys still don't want to admit they were beaten up by a girl because they think it makes them look like less of a man. They do what abused women do—excuses, rationalizing, whatever. You know the drill:

show up with flowers and candy—or, in the guy's case, beer—"

"Which he can't use in the hospital."

"Then, it's 'Oh, honey I don't know what came over me, I promise it'll never happen again.' I wonder how long the abuse was going on."

"Her beating him up or him beating her up?" Early asked.

"This isn't wrestling. Domestic violence isn't more acceptable when the combatants are evenly matched. Good thing they never had any kids." Hal chuckled. "Although their kid would have plenty of money for video games."

"And their kid would grow up to be just like them."

Hal stopped chuckling.

Now Early chuckled. "Siri 2.0. Or Chandler 2.0."

"Version One is bad enough. And no chance of ever getting the bugs out."

"Domestic abuse can escalate to murder. Don't people realize a gun has no gender?"

"Apparently, Hammond didn't," Hal said.

Early leaned back. "Do you believe anything Siri said during her interrogation?"

"She has no credibility with me. However, our good friend and District Attorney Tom Oud has the call on whether there's enough evidence to charge her with murder. I don't envy his having this crazy thing land in his lap."

"Are the two letters useful to him?" Early asked.

"I doubt they're sufficient to charge Siri with murder, but that's up to Tom. The lab found no identifiable prints on the camp letter. The Syria letter had plenty of them, but we can't confirm the writer because there were no matches in any of our databases. The prints on the cell phone also came up empty, but we were able to identify it as Hammond's from the content." Hal fast-forwarded the video and continued, "I was struck by the similarity of her demeanor in our video and in yours from the mansion. Her responses seem rehearsed in both of them. Watch what happens when he mentions the letter from Taziz again." Hal pressed play.

"I told you I don't know what the hell she's talking about," Siri snarled. "That little bitch robbed me, stole all our money, and my husband too."

Early remembered the Sneak Thief on the tarot card. *This case is full of thieves. And sneaks.*

"Taziz says he's dead and I killed him? Liar! If Chandler really is dead—oh my God." Siri sobbed into her hands. "You really think he's dead, don't you? You do. I hope it isn't true. But if he is . . ." She sniffled and carefully wiped her eyes with her palms to avoid smearing her mascara. "If he is then *she* must have killed him for the money."

Early found this interrogation more entertaining than television until he realized Siri wasn't going to give up anything useful. "Chief, if I listen to any more of this crap, I'll need a honey-dipper truck to clean out my ears."

"You should have seen her the first time he let her read Taziz's letter. It was ugly. Closely examine this room and you'll see the dents where she bounced off the walls."

"How did your poor detective keep from laughing? I'm glad I don't work for you."

"Me, too, although it would be the best job you ever had." Hal shut down the video player. "He's had lots of practice and this is all part of the job. Just like tough situations are part of your job too."

Early bit his lip. Time for another tough situation. "Hal . . . there's something I need to tell you."

Hal studied Early's face. "I didn't like the sound of that the last time you said it and I like it even less now."

"Me too, but it's important. Let's go into your office."

They walked through the squad room, Early taking in the sight of the officers at their desks. It felt good to be in a normal setting again. Seeing Siri in the interrogation tank was like watching a bad movie.

23

IN WHICH EARLY WAVES A RED FLAG IN FRONT OF THE CHIEF

Early closed the door to the Chief's office as Hal squeezed into his big leather chair. "Spit it out, Early."

"Like pulling a tooth?" Early plopped into another chair.

"I've seen quite enough teeth for a while. Some Maine champagne?" Hal pulled a bottle of coffee brandy and a couple of glasses from his desk drawer.

"Thanks, man." Early knocked back the drink Hal handed him. "Wait, cops can't drink on duty."

Hal grinned. "I officially declare myself off duty."

"You can do that while you're in your office?"

"It's good to be Chief." Hal took a snootful of brandy and replaced the bottle in his desk drawer. "Whatever you've got to say can't be that bad. Let's hear it."

Early looked at the floor. "You're not going to like this."

Hal folded his hands across his ample belly. "I dislike the whole situation. I dislike everybody in it. And I'm starting to dislike you. Stop farting around."

Early could see Hal wasn't playing. Best to get this over with. "After I snagged the flash drive at the mansion, I checked the safe for other interesting items."

Hal frowned. "If my men ever catch you, your ass is grass and I'm the lawnmower."

"I know. So, you can see the importance of what I'm going to tell you."

"Yes. Because you have a solid investigative background, I assume you have a damn good reason to think that confessing to burglary is your only way of telling me whatever it is you've got. I'm trusting your judgment. Don't make me regret it." He nodded. "Go on."

Relieved, Early continued. "I found a cooler."

"You found a cooler. In the safe." The Chief raised an eyebrow. "You pull off burglaries while you're drunk?"

"I was not drunk. I thought maybe I was crazy but there it was, under a blanket. It was too damn heavy to move but I could lift the lid enough to fit my hand inside."

"And what you felt in there was interesting enough to make you narc on yourself."

"Well, yeah. It was packed with plastic bags and something in one of them felt like a finger."

"A finger?" Hal crowed. "Right. Where in the hell did you get that idea?"

"It seemed to have a ring on it."

"Are you trying to make me puke?"

"Not deliberately. Should I wait until lunchtime?"

"Shut up. I mean, let's have the rest." Hal leaned back in his chair.

"While I was trying to sort things out, somebody unlocked the front door—"

"You tossed the place in the daytime?"

"No, it was well past midnight; I wasn't expecting anyone. I closed the safe and got out of the house before they came in."

"Did you see who the person was?" Hal asked.

"I didn't know at the time but I do now. It was Taziz."

"Great Hitchens' ghost! Was she alone or with Hammond?"

"Alone. She had come back for the money like she said in her letter. And she knew it was really in the floor safe," Early said.

"You saw her take the money?"

"No, but I saw her open the safe. I don't know how she figured out I was hiding in the bushes, but she pulled out a gun and started coming toward me. I thought it advisable to get the hell out of there."

"A wise policy," Hal said.

"I'm speculating that only Siri, Hammond, and Taziz knew about the floor safe. If Siri discovered the money was missing, she had to know only Taziz could have taken it since Hammond was long gone by then . . . one way or another. And because Hammond was very secretive, it's unlikely any of the staff even knew the safe existed let alone the combination. Siri told me she called Taziz when she couldn't reach Hammond, but Taziz had a cell phone under Hammond's account and the only incoming calls on her number were from France—presumably where her family is. Remember Taziz said that Siri told her to use Hammond's phone to make it look like he was still alive."

"The records back up Taziz's story. But what can I do with your other information? You're not positive you felt a finger in that cooler."

"Wait. You need to see this." Early commandeered the Chief's laptop to pull up the website of Siri's Seramics. Spectacular pottery images filled the screen. "Check out Siri's style. Pay particular attention to the colors."

"Early, what the hell? Now you're asking me to admire

Siri's pottery? Are you bucking to be the local newspaper's art critic?"

"Probably pays even worse than detective work. Notice how all her pots, plates, and mugs are glazed in muted shades of gray and brown."

"I can see that, Mr. Curator."

Early ran his finger across the screen. "There are lots of artistic touches too. Like the feathers on this one, the gold piping on these down here, the gemstones and beads on those others, and so on. Very subtle, pretty touches. It's characteristic of her older works as well as her newer ones." He pointed out the dates on each set of pictures.

"Got it, teach." Hal yawned and stretched. "When's the exam?"

"Now look at the pots she made during the month after Hammond's disappearance. She was working on some of them the first time I interviewed her and she explained her process to me quite extensively."

"After she beat you up." Hal chuckled.

"Leave the ball busting to Jeremy please." He clicked another link, flooding the screen with stunning pots glazed in swirling brilliant reds. "They're quite a departure from her usual style, wouldn't you say?"

"Yeah, really beautiful." Hal sat up, enchanted by the vibrant colors, and then asked, "But is this going somewhere?"

"Yes. I asked Amber if she could tell me where Hammond was."

"You consult psychics now?"

"I don't but she volunteered to help me out since we're in the same building."

"On the cheap side of town." Hal grinned.

"No that would be the police station."

Hal snorted. "Amber means well but she's never been much help to us."

"Hell, every PD should have a psychic."

"Why? None of my colleagues ever told me a psychic had helped them."

"Knowing how to handle people is the real advantage of a psychic. They're much better at it than cops are."

Because Hal tried to keep his mind open to all sides of an issue before forming an opinion, he contemplated Early's point of view. "Yeah, psychics might be better at telling people their loved ones are dead. Cops hate to do that. But as far as leads, all Amber ever seems to see is a cabin in the woods. And there aren't enough cops in Maine to cover all of those."

"Yes, she did say that. But more importantly, she saw red."

"She got mad?"

Early laughed. "No, she saw the color red."

"What was her explanation? Blood?"

"She couldn't come up with one. But here's why I don't think it was blood. You know how some professions have urban legends specific to them? Like police and airline pilots."

"Yeah, I remember one going around the stations in Philly about the perp whose coat got caught in the door of a cruiser. When the cop drove away and heard something banging against the car he stopped and found—"

"Um, tell me later," Early said. "And not during lunch, please. Anyway, pottery making is one of the oldest known art forms, going back to prehistory. Pottery artists like to experiment with various glaze additives to see their effects. I did some research on the ancient Asian technique Siri uses called raku and found some fascinating details on how each aspect of the process affects the finished product. I came upon a legend popular among pottery artists about an ancient Chinese potter who threw a pig into his kiln to see the effect on the glaze."

"Not the best use of one. I like animals even if they're uncooked."

"As the legend goes, when the potter finished his pots, they bore the most vibrant and unusual red coloring anyone had ever seen—"

"Like the red color Amber saw? And the colors on Siri's pots?"

"You're catching on." Early could almost see the Chief's mind assembling a jigsaw puzzle from the pieces he was giving Hal.

"The old potter throws a pig into the kiln with his pots," Hal said, "and the pig vaporizes or whatever and that turns the glaze red."

"Right. Then the king of China ordered the potter to produce the red pots exclusively. Unfortunately, the potter couldn't duplicate that exact red. He threw in more pigs, he tried other animals, but nothing worked."

"What's the connection to our case?"

"Because the potter suspected the king would have him beheaded for failing, he committed suicide by throwing himself into his kiln instead of waiting to be executed. But when his apprentices opened the kiln, guess what they found? A bunch of beautiful pots bearing the most striking red glaze they had ever seen."

Hal's eyes narrowed and darted from Early to the computer screen and back. Several times.

"Remember the tooth from Siri's ashes?" Early asked. "And Taziz said Siri kept repeating the word 'kill' after shooting Hammond? I think Taziz was wrong. I think Siri was saying 'kiln'."

"Great Hitchens' ghost, the potter threw himself into the kiln and the glaze turned red . . . Early, are you trying to tell me . . ." He pointed at the screen, his voice stuck in his throat.

Early couldn't remember when he'd seen the Chief speechless. Hal stared at the screen in silence, looks of horror and disgust chasing each other around his slack-jawed face. Early turned to him, his hand atop the screen filled with the images of Siri's bright red pots, and said, "Chief, I'm afraid we just found Chandler Hammond."

24

IN WHICH EARLY SEES MORE RED

"You think you've solved the case, eh?" Amber asked, shuffling her tarot cards. "Then, why ask me for another reading?"

"This whole thing is very bizarre. I still feel like I need some assurance," Early said.

"From the cards?"

"From anywhere. I'll take what I can get."

Amber snapped her chewing gum. "What was your conclusion?"

"This is just speculation," Early started, "but I think some of Crystalline's investors grew suspicious and started asking questions. Hammond got spooked and decided to disappear. After he caught his girlfriend and his wife together, he wisely figured he was better off without either one."

"Pretty smart for a man. I'm surprised he didn't try to figure out a way to keep both of them."

"Greed was his deadly sin. He stopped to get the money out of the safe."

"Do you think both Siri and Taziz knew Crystalline was a fraud?"

"Hammond's own company records prove that Taziz never supplied him with Iraqi artifacts. How could she think his company was legit if she knew he was lying about that?"

"Good point. Pull three cards." Amber fanned the deck across her reading table.

"Don't you want me to shuffle them?"

"I think you're too overwrought. We don't want to stress out the cards." Amber snickered.

Early pulled three cards and turned them face up as fast as he could.

Amber watched with intensity as he laid the cards down. When he pulled the first one, she chuckled. At the second, she laughed. By the time he flipped over the last one, she was roaring.

"What's so damn funny?" Early growled.

"I'm sorry." She gasped. "You have such a knack of picking the most appropriate cards."

"I do?" He peered at them. "With one exception, I don't see anything that looks very relevant."

"That's what readers are for. Take this first one." She held up the two of cups. "It's just a couple of people having a drink, right?"

Early nodded.

"Not hardly. In the deck this card falls between the Ace of Cups—starting something—and the three of cups—foolish pleasures. The man on the card is enticing the woman into something by appealing to her emotions. The figure rising out of the cups is the caduceus of Hermes who was widely known in Greece as the trickster god. Whatever this guy is proposing isn't on the up-and-up."

"Wow," Early said. "I never would have deduced that."

"I take it this card refers to Hammond's Ponzi scheme." She held up the second card. "This one is self-explanatory."

"The Fool." Early grinned. "It sure is."

"Over the centuries there have been many interpretations for the Fool, but it's a no-brainer in this reading."

"And the last card? Why did that make you lose it?"

She placed her hand on the Page of Cups. "Pages are one of the more mysterious figures in the deck. Some say they evolved into the jack of modern playing cards and some say jacks came from the knights in the tarot. Others say knights and pages merged to become the jacks. You can see their history is rather hazy."

Early grimaced. "Just like this case."

"But check this page out: he's holding a cup and a surprise just popped out of it—a fish. He wasn't expecting that."

"Why is it funny?"

"Don't you get it? You told me where you think Hammond's remains came to rest . . . so to speak."

"Yes. In Siri's pottery."

"Pottery such as a cup."

The dawn rose on Early's face. "Yeah, and that's a surprise to everybody."

Amber started laughing again. "Although this cup looks more like metal, I'd say the card confirms your idea."

Early sat back. "Thanks, Amber. Believe it or not, this is a relief."

Amber gathered up the deck. "You really think Siri murdered him? He didn't just take off with his girlfriend like everybody said?"

"Oh yeah. Hammond was the rainmaker for the Ponzi scheme. If he left by whatever means, the gravy train went with him. After Siri killed him, she came up with the story that he and Taziz had absconded with the company funds to avoid paying restitution to all the victims."

"And everyone in Finderne bought it."

"Except Honoria. Regardless of who killed Hammond, somebody had to dismember the body because Siri's kiln isn't big enough to accommodate a corpse. I think she locked that cooler I mentioned to you in the safe to keep anyone from discovering what was left of poor old Hammond."

"Gross. The red I saw in my vision must have been Siri's pottery glaze."

"Or Hammond's blood, which would have melted along with the snow. At the very least, Hammond's girlfriend, Taziz, helped Siri dispose of something—the body, the evidence, or both. Why let a good corpse go to waste? Make pottery glaze."

"Not a bad use of a financier," Amber reflected. "How could I have missed all this excitement in those readings I did for you? Guess I need to hone my craft a little better." She cocked her head. "Do you hear somebody outside?"

Footsteps came down the hall followed by the sound of Early's office door opening. He jumped from his chair and dashed out of Amber's reading room to find Tikki and George standing wide-eyed in his doorway. "What are you kids doing here?"

"George wanted to see Private-Eye-Land," Tikki said.

Early turned to look through the front door of the waiting room. "And how did you get here?"

"George drove."

"Oh yeah? Where did he get a car?"

"I just borrowed it from the house across the street from yours," George said.

Early's jaw dropped. "Great Hitchens' ghost, you stole my neighbor's car?"

George smiled. "Nah. We're gonna return it when we get back."

"George, I will not have you being a bad influence on Tikki."

"Aw Dad, somebody should be," said Tikki.

Early rolled his eyes. "Tikki, you told me you had no wish, want, or desire to steal a car."

"That was then . . ."

"I'm not having a live action version of *Grand Theft Auto* in our hood."

Wah-wok, wah-wah-wok. The theme from *Shaft* sprang from Early's pocket and he dug out his phone. "Ah, a message from the Chief—he's found you a spot at a residential facility over in Derry, George. You can move in there tomorrow."

George grimaced. "Is it better than home was?"

"Probably. At least nobody will shoot at you." Early scrolled through his phone listings. "I hope I have our neighbor's number in here. And knock off stealing cars, George. We're not in Portland, ya know."

25

IN WHICH THE BIG THREE CONFERENCE IS HELD

Sleepy-eyed Early found himself at Throw the Book again. He wasn't sure how many more of these crack-of-dawn meetings he could take. Maine may be the first state to greet the sunrise but he saw no reason to be awake when it happened.

Hal was at his usual table with District Attorney Tom Oud. Both were staring at the Chief's laptop. Hal pointed to the screen. "That is *so gross.*"

Tom sat back and took a sip of coffee. "Absurd."

The Chief tossed a piece of paper at him. "The legend of the raku pig. Read it and weep."

Tom was reading but not weeping as Early walked up and glanced at the screen. "Oh, you're checking out Siri's pottery."

"I explained your theory to Tom between ice fishing stories," Hal said.

Early tilted his head. "You don't ice fish. You don't even regular fish."

"Yeah, but I like to hear all the creative ways that people fix up their ice fishing shacks."

Tom laughed and shook Early's hand. "I'm sorry about this breakfast meeting, Early, but my schedule's packed." He pulled his tablet from his spiffy leather briefcase. "I find your theory about this alleged murder case intriguing."

Early signaled to Jerry for coffee and sat down. "Hell, Hal's told me worse stories at this very table—things we know really happened."

"But they didn't happen in Finderne," the Chief exclaimed, nearly gagging. "This is local. And disgusting. The question is do we have enough evidence to prove a murder at all, much less whom to prosecute?"

"That," Tom said, "is what brings us here at this ghastly hour. I figured you two would rather not be quite awake when I broke the unpleasant news."

"Food helps," the Chief said, munching a blueberry muffin.

"Let me guess. You're not gonna charge Siri with murder, right?" Early muttered as he sipped his coffee.

Tom looked at Hal. "He's good."

"Sometimes," the Chief said after a burp.

"I'm afraid we just ain't got it." Tom shook his head. "No evidence that a murder even occurred much less whodunit. And this ancient Chinese raku legend stuff isn't evidence, it's crap." He flipped the paper back to the Chief.

"I hate to say that's what I've thought all along," the Chief said. "I was hoping you would prove me wrong."

"Wish I could." The district attorney sighed. "Considering what we now know about Crystalline, I agree that Chandler Hammond's disappearance stinks to high heaven. But homicide? I couldn't put together a case based on what you gave me."

"Even with the body parts in the cooler?" Early asked.

Tom scowled. "That's just speculation on your part. Furthermore, do you really wanna confess to burglary?"

Early swirled his coffee, staring into his cup. "Why not confiscate the cooler now and test for traces of Hammond's DNA?"

Tom rolled his eyes. "We're gonna find Hammond's DNA in his own cooler? Ya think?"

"How about using Luminol to look for blood traces?" Early asked.

"You know Luminol picks up other kinds of stains too. Didn't Siri say she stored her glaze additives in there?" Tom said.

"Now that you mention it, she did say she used manure and I know Luminol picks that up." Early frowned. "But why stash a cooler full of glaze additives in a safe?"

"We don't know *what* was in the cooler," Tom continued. "You couldn't conclusively identify the contents of the bags. They could have held . . . well . . . pig parts."

"Something sure felt like a finger to me."

"Or a pig tail," Tom said.

"With a ring on it?" Early said.

Tom shrugged. "A pet pig whose owner liked Goth piercings?"

Early did a facepalm. "Whose side are you on, Tom?"

The district attorney laughed, tilted his chair back, and ran his fingers through his wild brown hair. "Sorry, Early. I'm on yours. You know that. Otherwise, I'd be prosecuting you for certain unmentionable acts in connection with this case—and who knows how many others."

Early shook his head. "If they were pig parts, why was the cooler in the safe? Did it stink too much to keep in the refrigerator?"

"Whatever reason Siri had for that," Tom went on, "the

cooler is either empty or missing. In either case, we have no way of determining what its contents were."

"And the red pottery glaze?" Early pointed at the scarlet pots on the screen. "That's a complete departure from Siri's usual style. We know what can produce such a unique color—"

"We know no such thing," the Chief interrupted. "You're basing that on a legend."

"But its sudden appearance on her pots coincides with Hammond's disappearance. That isn't probable cause?" Early asked.

"Ah, the color of pottery glaze as probable cause." Tom sighed, hands behind his head. "About as solid as basing the color on a legend, isn't it? The idea of Siri using her husband's corpse as a glaze component might make sense to you Early, but it's pure conjecture." He gestured toward Hal. "We're not pottery experts. During all my years in law enforcement, I've never even heard of a forensic potter. We have no idea how she produced that color or why she diverged from her usual style. Hell, she might have used a real pig. And even if she did throw Chandler Hammond into the kiln, it's impossible to isolate and identify human remains in a glaze."

Early slumped over. "You sound like a public defender."

"I'll have to cop to that charge this time. Maybe we can come up with a whole new category of homicide. How about murder by red pottery glaze? We could call it . . . Redrum," Tom said.

Hal groaned. "You have the right to remain silent."

"The right but not the desire." Tom grinned. "Guys, it's my job to weigh all sides. Although Early's theory sounds eerily plausible to me, that's all it is—a theory."

"Can you imagine if the media got hold of this? I can

envision the tabloids overrunning town trying to dig up juicy tidbits on the Finderne Pottery Murder. The media will have enough on their plates with the Crystalline Ponzi scheme. Finderne will be famous," Hal crowed.

"I'm actually looking forward to seeing Crystalline in court because it won't be my court." Tom chuckled. "Club Fed can have this one."

"Siri never thought Taziz would double-cross her," Early went on, "but Taziz didn't want to share a murder rap."

"Taziz doesn't even realize nobody thinks Hammond is dead," Hal said. "She's hiding out from us for nothing."

Tom shoved his tablet into his briefcase. "That remains to be seen. But for proof of homicide, we don't have squat and obtaining a murder conviction without a body is practically impossible."

"It's been done in Maine," Hal objected.

"Those convictions were based on bulletproof forensic evidence, and we have nothing rising to that caliber, so to speak." Tom began ticking on his fingers. "We've got a letter from Taziz, which may be largely a fairy tale. We can't even substantiate she wrote it. We have a fragment of another letter that was burned beyond any possibility of establishing the writer or intended recipient. We have no murder weapon."

"If Siri shot Hammond and dumped the gun in the drink, I'd bet on the Kennebec," Hal postulated. "It runs fast and deep and I'm sure there's plenty of stuff in there that the cops would love to fish out."

"Such things would be of interest to the district attorney's office too," Tom said. "Maybe I'll fish out something of the sort at the reach next week, although I'd prefer fish. But to continue: we have a tooth, which could have been lost by ordinary means."

"If you consider a punch in the mouth ordinary means," Early grumbled.

"It's ordinary for some people." Tom snickered.

Early shuddered. "Considering how easily Siri admitted to domestic violence, she probably *could* chop Hammond up."

"Bitter experience tells me her explanation of how the tooth got into the ashes would be just good enough to create reasonable doubt in a jury," said Tom.

"This sucks," Early groaned.

"That's something we all agree on," said Tom swiftly. "There's the Bentley abandoned at the airport. Or not. And lastly, a cooler stashed in a safe containing unidentifiable contents, which are now missing." He threw up his hands. "The whole damn case is missing. We can spin endless scenarios and we may even get some things right. But nothing we've got even comes close to being evidence of a crime. *Any* crime."

"We can't even prove Hammond took the dirt nap," the Chief said. "He could be hiding out in Argentina."

"Don't cry for him." Early chortled.

"The news isn't all grim," Tom continued. "Because the flash drive containing Crystalline's corporate records may be evidence of fraud the feds were salivating to pounce on it for forensic accounting."

"That's what I'm talking about," Hal said.

"I'll shoot you a status update as soon as I get one from my contacts. For now, good morning gentlemen." Tom smiled, picked up his briefcase, and sauntered out the front door.

"Now what?" Early asked.

The Chief closed his laptop and rose. "Now you gotta

break all this to Honoria. She's probably dialing your number as we speak."

26

IN WHICH EARLY BECOMES A PLANT MANAGER

Another spring, another mud season. Despite its nickname, spring in Maine is always welcome. Eager gardeners rush to plant seeds in cold frames and hoop houses. Ladyslippers flash their round, pink bellies in bawdy joy delighting hikers in the woods.

The winter had been harsh and long, but now Early shared in the budding spirit by planning a new garden. "Tikki," he yelled from garden headquarters also known as the kitchen table. "Did you plant the lettuce yet?"

"I'm putting the seeds into the window box right now."

While thumbing through a seed catalog for ideas, Early came across lush pictures of irises like the ones his wife had planted by their front porch years ago. Soon, the white and purple flowers would sprout, bringing back memories of her.

"Tikki!"

"What?" Tikki walked in the door, holding a trowel in his dirty hands.

"Don't get mud on the floor."

"I'll clean it later," his son snapped. "Whaddaya want?"

"Don't yell at me," Early yelled.

"I'll never finish planting if you keep interrupting me."

Early sighed. "Sorry. I was just . . ."

Tikki glimpsed the iris pictures and understood. Grasping for a distraction he leaned over his father's garden container diagram. "Looks like a good layout for the deck. Did you decide what to plant yet?"

"As many veggies as we can fit." Early laughed. "Lettuce, tomatoes, cukes, maybe some herbs, and—oh did you start the spinach?"

"Spinach is *hard,*" Tikki moaned.

"It's fussy. Too much water, not enough water, too much sun, not enough sun, too cold, too hot. Hitting the right balance is tough. Kinda like life ya know?"

"We could just buy it in the supermarket. That would be a lot less work."

"Perennials are easier. Why not try asparagus?" Early asked.

"I would if I liked it."

"You can learn to like all kinds of things when that means less work."

Tikki considered this for a moment and said, "Got any ideas to make spinach less work?"

"Sprout the seeds in a wet paper towel. That will tell you which ones are viable."

"I'll try it," his son said, walking out the door.

Returning to the iris pictures brought Early's thoughts back to his runaway wife. He had tried everything he could think of to get her to come home but nothing had worked. He needed to stop blaming himself for her departure. What to do? *First, I'm gonna buy a bunch of flowers to plant around those damn irises and hide them.*

He pulled on a jacket and jumped into his Caprice.

Pebbles from the driveway flew everywhere as he tore off to the garden center. But when he walked into the center he froze. The place was full of irises.

He felt haunted by irises. All too soon he would have to walk past them whenever he came home—a constant reminder of his wife. Still, he couldn't bring himself to pull them out. *Maybe I should use the back door? Nah, we've made too much social progress for that.*

He decided to browse whatever was farthest from the irises. Soon a raft of primroses smiled up at him. Early smiled back. He loved their sweet little faces and many were perennials, which should please Tikki. He knelt beside the primrose flats, soaking up the colors, choosing plants of crimson and blue. Suddenly, his train of thought was derailed by a big booming voice.

"Early!"

He looked up to see the Chief walking towards him.

"Hey, Hal. Martha assigned you to garden duty today?"

"She does her garden duty; I do mine. Darren and I are looking for spinach seedlings."

"If by some miracle you find them please let my son know."

"He's still trying to grow spinach from seed?" Hal asked.

"It's a challenge. Some folks got it, some folks ain't."

"Early, sometimes you're just mean. Lighten up."

"Can't. I was born this color."

"Me too." Hal chuckled. "Tikki will just have to learn by trial and error, like most of us."

"What have you learned? How to scam your wife into going to the farmer's market every week?"

"You're such a comedian. I wish you were on TV. Like that local late-night talk show host with the big ears."

Early's eyebrows rose. "You think I'm that funny?"

"No, but at least I could shut you off." The Chief slapped Early's shoulder. "I wanted to tell you we got good news about the Hammond case down at the station this morning."

Early grinned so wide a sunbeam could have sprung from his mouth. "What is it?"

"Tom Oud says his contact gave him an update about the investigation into Crystalline."

"That's your good news?"

"Don't rush me." Hal raised his eyes to the skies. "I'm savoring the moment. The feds think that Siri attempted to divert investor suspicion by lying about Hammond's disappearance. Specifically, his Bentley being at the airport. They spent a whole day studying the parking lot security videos you and Tikki went over and they never saw his car."

"We could have saved them the trouble."

"They're the feds. They don't want you to save them the trouble. But wait, it gets better." The Chief smiled, and then continued, "Turns out that Crystalline was Hammond *and* Siri's company. After the feds did forensic accounting on Crystalline's records and interviewed investors they discovered Siri was quite a bit more involved in the company than she let on. And since Hammond's not around she has to deal with the whole mess herself."

Early busted out laughing. When he regained his composure he asked, "What's Crystalline's status?"

"It's been designated a Ponzi scheme or whatever they officially call that kinda thing. And remember that letter to Larry Bloch that Tikki found? Turns out he's involved in money laundering. After they arrested him he confessed to exchanging checks and money orders from Hammond for cash. He quickly rolled over on Hammond, Siri, and Taziz."

Early got excited. "Do they think Siri killed Hammond?"

"Nah, they think he's hiding out somewhere. They even think she knows where he is. She tried to use the Bentley as a red herring, but it ended up biting her in the end. Once the feds discovered she lied about the Bentley, they started digging to find out what else she lied about. We think she's lying because of murder, but the feds think she's lying because of fraud and they have the better case."

"Having to tow a Bentley is suspicious all by itself," Early murmured, stroking the fuzzy yellow petals of a primrose.

"What did you end up telling Honoria?" Hal asked.

"Mostly the truth: we don't know whether Hammond's still alive. I didn't tell her we think Siri murdered Hammond because we could still be wrong. I figured she'd think I was full of shit and I felt bad about that until she threw me out of the house."

"Great Hitchens' ghost," the Chief said. "She must have been really pissed."

"She did have quite a hissy fit, but she called later and apologized."

"She doesn't know how lucky she was," Hal said.

"What do you mean?"

"Tom said the feds became suspicious when they found she was the only person on the investor list who had ever received dividends. Being a member of the family made it look even worse for her since many times they're in on the scam. They called her in for questioning with the stipulation that she prove she was an investor and not a party to the fraud."

"That must have set her off louder than the Fourth of July." Early snickered.

"I don't envy *that* interrogation."

"She asked that I continue trying to find her brother. Like I feared, this has become a zombie case. But I agreed anyway—searching for him won't interfere with my regular work, what there is of it. Plus, I can pick up some spare change." Early smiled. "And you never know, Hal, someday we might figure out what really did happen to Chandler Hammond."

"If you can prove he was murdered, Honoria could sue Siri for wrongful death like the Goldmans did to O.J."

Early snorted. "I'll probably never be able to prove it since we figure he's in Siri's pottery." He looked up at Hal. "Did the feds find anything in the big safe besides the flash drive when they raided the place?"

"No."

"They checked thoroughly?"

"Early, they're the feds. Of course, they did." Suddenly, Hal understood. "No cooler. Are you sure you didn't hallucinate that? Did you smoke anything before you broke in?"

"Great Hitchens' ghost, first you say I was drunk and now you accuse me of being stoned? Don't interrogate me like a perp."

"Why not? You were a perp that night. You even confessed to an officer of the law."

"Arrest me already." Early frowned. "I wonder if Hammond had life insurance. That's always a good motive for murder."

"Well, you know the insured has to actually be dead for the beneficiary to collect. And the very thing keeping Siri out of jail on a first-degree murder charge keeps her from collecting the insurance—no proof of death. She may not be the sharpest knife in the drawer, but she wouldn't cop to murder just to cash in a policy."

"She could have him declared dead but that would take years. Talk about shooting yourself in the foot."

"We both think her foot wasn't what she shot." Hal's eyes

sparkled. "Wouldn't it be a hoot if Hammond had a ton of life insurance and Taziz was the beneficiary?"

Early and the Chief roared with laughter.

"But wait there's more." Hal wiped his eyes. "Here's the best part: not only is Siri looking at possible jail time for money laundering and tax evasion, the feds froze all her assets and confiscated her kiln as evidence."

Early put down the primrose he was holding, so his laughing wouldn't shake it out of its pot. "Sweet. The Hammond money train is a complete wreck."

"I'm not a big believer in karma but this is just too rich. We done good bruh. We should celebrate over lunch."

"Only if lunch is on you this time. And none of those damn gross-out cop stories."

"I promise. I'm gonna go see if Darren found any seedlings. By the way, there are all kinds of tomatoes here." The Chief waved toward a faraway area of the capacious greenhouse as he walked away. "Get your black ass over to the vegetable section."

Early turned back to the primroses, happy to know some good had come out of the Crystalline quagmire. Siri had escaped a murder rap, but she was dead broke and probably headed to the slammer. He figured that was fitting justice for a woman who murdered for money and then let her husband go to pot.

THE LEGEND OF THE RAKU PIG

IN WHICH POTTERY ARTISTS PIG OUT.

Many centuries ago in China, there lived a Potter who worked for the King. He wanted to please his monarch by producing the most beautifully glazed pottery of all the potters in the land. In his efforts to accomplish this, he experimented by putting many different kinds of additives into his kiln with the graceful pots he fired every day.

One day, he was having great difficulty with his process. None of the glazes he tried were coming out the way he wanted. He decided to try something different and put a pig into the kiln. When the pots were finished firing, he pulled open the door of his kiln and there stood the most beautiful blood-red glazed pottery he had ever beheld. No one across the entire kingdom had ever seen such a color on a pot before.

When the King of China saw the great beauty of the pots, he ordered them broken into pieces and the pieces set into rings for everyone in his court. Then, the King demanded that the Potter produce more of the blood-red glazed pots for him.

Much to his dismay, the Potter discovered he was unable

to reproduce that exact red glaze. He tried putting another pig into the kiln with the next batch of pots, but the results were disappointing and he destroyed the pots. He checked his formulas over and over but could find no discrepancies to explain the problem. After trying everything he could think of, he still had no success in reproducing the blood-red glaze the King had admired.

Meanwhile, the King grew impatient and decreed that the Potter should make only the blood-red glaze pots and no others or the consequences would be dire. Fearing for his life, the Potter worked night and day to replicate his initial success but was still unable to achieve his goal. At last, after countless failures, the day came when out of sheer despair the old Potter decided that his life was over. Rather than submit to a beheading by the King, he threw himself into the kiln with his pots and pulled the door closed behind him. When his apprentices opened the kiln afterward, they gazed in wonder for there stood the blood-red glaze pots more stunning than ever. But the Potter never saw his work for he had burnt up in the fire and become part of the blood-red glaze.

ACKNOWLEDGMENTS

This book would not have been possible without the friendship and guidance of my technical advisor Christine Barath, intuitive medium and owner of EarthMagic Pottery. I also wish to thank my two beta readers: my husband Paul (who doesn't like my work) and my best friend Sharon Kolbek (who does). Much gratitude goes to two editors who gave me encouragement when I needed it, Anita Bunkley and Barbara Rogan. Finally, I am grateful for the support of all my good friends, who have been eagerly waiting to read this book!

ABOUT THE AUTHOR

Roslyn lives with her corgi, Great Pyrenees, and husband in Downeast Maine, where she gardens, lifts weights, hikes, and renovates houses.

Follow Roslyn on Twitter at @the_moonshadow

Made in the USA
Lexington, KY
25 November 2019

57588170R00131